TREACHEROUS TRAIL

When the son of wealthy El Paso banker Rufas McCabe was kidnapped in broad daylight, McCabe believed that all he must do was pay the ransom in order to return everything to normality. He was very wrong. The ruthless outlaws, led by the infamous Big Bill O'Mara, had no intention of returning Joseph McCabe so easily, not when they could milk the old banker dry. All seemed lost until ex-lawman Cal Hayes entered the picture. If anyone could track down the gang and their hostage, it was Hayes.

TREACHEROUS TRAIL

TREACHEROUS TRAIL

by

John Ladd

Dales Large Print Books
Long Preston, North Yorkshire,
BD23 4ND, England.

British Library Cataloguing in Publication Data.

Ladd, John
  Treacherous trail.

    A catalogue record of this book is
    available from the British Library

    ISBN   1-84262-350-8 pbk

First published in Great Britain 2004 by Robert Hale Limited

Copyright © John Ladd 2004

Cover illustration © Prieto by arrangement with
Norma Editorial S.A.

Published in Large Print 2005 by arrangement with
Robert Hale Ltd.

Dales Large Print is an imprint of Library Magna Books Ltd.

Printed and bound in Great Britain by
T.J. (International) Ltd., Cornwall, PL28 8RW

*Dedicated to Lewis and Billy,
the Williams brothers.*

ONE

The sun had set a few hours earlier but the lone rider had continued spurring his mount on. There was no moon for the coyotes to howl at, only a million stars casting their eerie light across the overhanging trees and the dusty trail that curled its way between them.

The horseman had not seen another living soul for more than five days and yet he seemed unable to rest. Unable to relax. It was as though he imagined death lurked in every shadow. For he had known death to stalk him from far less ominous places in the past. Without even knowing why, he forced the horse on as if either afraid or unwilling to make camp.

The rider did not know this land and what he did not know, he could never trust. It was

1000 miles from where his journey had originally started. Eight years of heading constantly westward had sharpened his instincts, but allowed his fears to grow unchecked with each new mile which past beneath the hoofs of his black stallion.

But Cal Hayes was no aimless drifter.

He had proved that many times.

He had become a skilled gunfighter, not through choice, but necessity. Over the years he tried his hand at most jobs there were to be had in the ever-changing place known simply as the West. But it was his mastery of the seven-inch barrelled silver-plated Colt Peacemaker that rested in his holster which had allowed him to survive.

Hayes knew how to use that skill to make himself money and fill his belly. He had been a deputy more times than he could recall, and hired himself out to whoever was willing to pay his price. That was why he was here now riding through the heavily wooded mountains towards a destination of which he had only second-hand knowledge.

He had been hired by the El Paso banker, Rufas McCabe, to locate his kidnapped son, Joseph. A ransom had already been paid and collected long before Hayes had been given the job of trying to track down either the eighteen-year-old or his capturers.

It was a mission Hayes had originally declined, but the generous $1000 advance fee had made the rider defy his own judgement and instincts. He knew that the chances of finding Joseph McCabe alive were slim, if not non-existent.

Cal Hayes tapped his spurs into the lathered hide of his horse and urged the faithful mount on up the tree-lined trail towards the dusty crest.

There was nothing to see except the blackness which surrounded him, yet Hayes knew that a million dangers could hide in those shadows.

This land was unlike anything he had encountered on his long journey. There was something about it that chilled him to the marrow. Maybe it was the tall straight trees which seemed to touch the clouds, or the uneasy silence that had surrounded him for days, that troubled him.

Whatever it was, Hayes rode on and on as if knowing that he would not willingly stop on the dusty trail that wound its way through the otherwise lush landscape until he found something resembling a town.

Cal Hayes steered his tired mount up the steep incline until at last he reached the high crest. Then he hauled in his reins and looked all around him. He could see the starlight sparkling off the tips of countless trees below him. Hayes took his canteen in his hands and unscrewed its stopper. He drank the last of his water and stared down from his high vantage point.

The sight below suddenly made him forget the black trees which flanked both sides of the rugged trail. A sprawling town lay a mere half-mile below him. For a moment he felt relieved that he had at last found a place where he might find a bed to rest his aching bones for what remained of the night. Hayes returned the canteen to the saddle horn, tapped his spurs into the horse and encouraged it down towards the scores of buildings.

The closer he got to the town, the more he noticed that something was wrong. The hair on the nape of his neck tingled beneath his sweat-soaked bandanna.

At first glance the town appeared deserted to the tall rider who steered his horse through the dark streets, his left hand holding his reins whilst his right wrist rested on the pearl-handled gun grip poking out of his holster.

Hayes's eyes flashed around him at the sparse rays of light that managed to escape from shuttered windows and ill-fitting door-frames of the various buildings and splash out on to the empty streets. As the sound of his horse's hoofs echoed around the wooden buildings, even those lights disappeared.

There were people here, Hayes thought. Terrified people.

There was no noise within the boundaries

of the town apart from that of his walking horse. Not a single other sound reached the ears of the tense horseman.

He was not the nervous sort, but this town made him skittish and he did not like the feeling. Hayes had not felt at ease in himself since entering this strange territory and now the first town he had discovered within its borders was adding to his worries.

Hayes allowed the long-legged black stallion to turn into the town's third street and continue walking. This street was as deserted as the first two, but he wondered how many people were hiding behind its locked doors, and why?

His eyes darted from one street-lantern to another. None of them was lit. That too made him wonder why? He had passed three saloons so far and each had its doors locked. Sweat began to trace its way down the middle of his broad back beneath his shirt.

The rider's right thumb flicked the safety loop off his Colt Peacemaker, then his index finger slid into the metal trigger guard. He stroked the trigger as his mount continued walking.

Whatever the fearful citizens of this town were afraid of might make them start shooting whatever weaponry they had, in his direction.

He could smell the danger that this town posed to him with every beat of his pounding heart, but he could not stop and turn his mount around and simply ride away. He was committed and he knew it. Hayes had to keep going however great the danger might be.

The rider bit his lip and allowed his eyes to flash from one shadow to the next.

Hayes knew that none of this made any sense.

Rufas McCabe had told him to expect a town on the long trail but not one like this!

Where were the townsfolk? Were they all hiding inside the buildings, or were those other people? People who had good reason to remain behind locked doors.

Could he have located the kidnappers? If so, it had been too easy. Far too easy!

Hayes noticed something else that concerned him.

So far he had not seen a solitary horse within the boundaries of the nameless town. But he could sure smell them. They were here somewhere, but for some strange reason they too were hidden from view.

Why?

Hayes looked up at the balconies of various larger buildings and tried to focus through the darkness. With only the light of countless stars above him, it was not easy to see anything, but he knew there were eyes watching him.

He instinctively felt them watching his every move.

Their fear was now chilling him.

What were they hiding from and why?

He slowed the horse up at a water trough and allowed the stallion to drink. He glanced around at the buildings opposite him. They were big. One was a gambling-hall and the other a well-maintained hotel.

Both were shrouded in shadow.

Hayes teased back on his reins and squinted across into the dark, almost impenetrable shadows to his right. Something had caught his eye on the porch of the hotel, but he was unsure what it was. He stroked the neck of the tired stallion and wondered if it might have been a firefly.

Or was his tired mind simply fashioning images that only existed in his primed imagination?

Then he saw it again.

This time there was no mistake. It was real.

Along the side of the hotel boardwalk a single glowing red ember brightened the darkness every few seconds.

That was no firefly.

Someone was sucking on a cigar.

Cal Hayes pulled the brim of his Stetson down and stared at the single red dot. It moved around, letting the rider know that whoever it was in the shadows, he was removing the smoke from his lips every few seconds to flick the ash off.

It became clear by the height of the hot burning ember that the smoker was seated.

Hayes kept his hand on his Colt and then hauled his reins to the right. He gently spurred and allowed the stallion to walk towards the only sign of life he had so far found in this silent town.

As the tall horse drew closer to the hotel's hitching post, Cal Hayes detected the aroma of a fine Havana on the night air.

Whoever it was, he was smoking a very expensive cigar.

'Stop right there, stranger.' The voice came a fraction of a second after the rider had heard the unmistakable sound of a gun hammer being locked into position.

Hayes obeyed the command, halted his mount and swallowed hard.

There was no time to haul his own weapon from its holster. No time to do anything with a target that he had not yet seen. All he could do was comply with the order. The sound of the pistol being primed had ensured that.

This was a voice that you took seriously.

'You have me at a disadvantage, partner,' Cal Hayes said in a low tone.

'Damn right!' the voice agreed. 'One false move and I'll blast a hole right through your middle.'

'I'm too tired to do anything,' Hayes retorted.

'Good. You might just live a tad longer,' the voice said coldly.

The rider began to sweat hard. He knew that there was no way he would be able to clear his holster with his Peacemaker before the man squeezed his trigger and blasted a hole right through him.

Hayes cleared his throat. 'Is that a Smith and Wesson you got aimed at me?'

'Yep. A Smith and Wesson Schofield .45, to be exact,' the voice confirmed. 'You got a good ear.'

The horseman held his nervous horse in check.

'I heard tell that Jake and Frank Ritter use Schofields. Reckon they must be mighty good guns for them boys to use them.'

'Frank'll use anything with bullets in it.' The sound of a chair creaking told Hayes that the man was on the rise. The barrel of the gun was suddenly illuminated by the starlight. It was aimed straight at his middle by a hand that was small but confident.

The mounted man licked his dry lips and saw the vague outline of the face before him. It was a face that he had seen a hundred times on Wanted posters over the years. Its handsome features were almost too perfect for someone who had made his living from robbery and killing for over half a decade.

'But you're right about me; I do prefer the Schofield.'

'Jake Ritter!' Cal Hayes muttered the name under his breath.

'Right again, stranger.'

TWO

The sound of his pounding heart almost deafened the rider opposite Jake Ritter. If there was one man whom you did not want to bump into in the middle of the night, it was the cold-eyed Ritter. Yet that was who Cal Hayes had somehow managed to find himself facing.

The starlight illuminated the sturdy Smith & Wesson pistol in the outlaw's hand with an unnerving clarity.

Hayes carefully eased himself off his saddle and slowly lowered his long right leg to the ground. He held on to the saddle horn firmly with both hands so that the deadly outlaw with the Schofield trained on him would not think that he was going for the Colt Peacemaker sitting in his hand-tooled holster.

The blue-steel barrel of the gun followed

Hayes's every movement.

Hayes inhaled deeply and tilted his head to look at the expressionless face of his adversary. He slowly released his grip on the saddle horn and kept his hands high as he squared up to the watchful Ritter.

'What's going on here?' Hayes asked.

Ritter gestured to the hitching pole.

'Tie that nag up, stranger. Good and tight.'

Hayes bit his lower lip again and did exactly as he was instructed. Then he looked up at the thin figure on the boardwalk above him. Jake Ritter looked nothing like a killer and yet Hayes knew that he was. The almost childlike features belied a man who had ridden with the infamous Quantrill Raiders during the War.

There was no brutality beyond that bunch, and Hayes knew it. They had become killing machines and Jake Ritter was one of the best of them.

If not *the* best.

No viciousness was beyond this angelic-looking devil.

Cal Hayes tightened the knot of his reins, then rested his rump against the hitching pole and carefully pushed his Stetson off his face.

'I'll ask you again, Jake. What's going on?'

Ritter waved the barrel of his gun.

'Get up here.'

Hayes exhaled heavily and stepped up on to the boardwalk porch of the hotel. He paused beside the outlaw and looked into the glistening eyes. He wondered how many men had stared into those innocent-looking eyes and then been savagely slain? If all the stories were true, it had not just been men who had been killed by Jake Ritter.

'What you want me to do now?' Hayes asked quietly.

Ritter rammed the barrel of the Schofield hard into Hayes's ribs and kept it there.

'Walk.'

Hayes turned and began to walk. Every step was matched with the barrel's being thrust into the back of his ribs.

'Where we going?' Hayes winced.

Ritter pushed the pistol even harder into the taller man's back.

'You ask too many damn questions, stranger. It can be a fatal habit, ya know?'

Cal Hayes continued walking. He knew that at least one of his ribs must have been cracked and did not want to give the outlaw an excuse to bust any more. He gritted his teeth and remained silent. The two men walked along the boardwalk past a dozen chairs towards a doorway at the side of the hotel.

Even in the darkness, Hayes could make out its shape due to the white-paint trim that edged it.

Hayes stopped walking when the brim of his hat touched the door. He felt the gun pressing through his sweat-soaked shirt, just above his belt. If Ritter squeezed the trigger of his Schofield now, he would sever his spine in two, Hayes thought.

'Open the door,' Ritter ordered.

Hayes slowly lowered his left arm and then

held on to the brass doorhandle. He turned it and felt the lock release.

'Now go inside,' Ritter growled in a low voice.

Again, he obeyed.

It was even darker in the room than it was outside the hotel, Hayes thought as he carefully edged inside. The shutters were closed tight and not one glint of starlight could penetrate its blackness. A multitude of thoughts raced through Hayes's mind.

What was Jake Ritter doing here? Were the rest of his gang with him? Was he going to kill him here and now?

Cal Hayes stopped when he heard the door being closed behind them. Every sinew in his body told him that he ought to turn and draw on the infamous outlaw, but he knew what would happen if he did. No man could manage that feat when Ritter already had his beloved Schofield in his hand.

There was a fine line between courage and suicide. Hayes was determined not to cross that line.

Ritter struck a match and touched the wick of a candle on a table in the centre of the room. The light suddenly allowed both men to see one another clearly for the first time. Neither seemed to enjoy the experience.

'You bother me, stranger,' Ritter said. He blew out the match and studied the dust-caked rider.

Hayes turned slowly until his whole body was facing the outlaw. He glanced down at the gun in Ritter's hand for a brief moment. It was still aimed at his belly.

'I ain't looking for no trouble, Jake.'

'You expect me to believe that eyewash? With a fancy shooting-rig like that strapped to your hip, you ain't looking for no ranch work.' Ritter's face was still totally expressionless. Words fell from the thin lips but the rest of the face did not show any emotion at all.

'I'm a gunfighter. A hired gun,' Hayes said. 'I ain't no bounty hunter.'

'Now we seem to be getting to the truth.' Ritter nodded. 'Have I heard of you? What do they call you?'

Hayes felt his heart starting to pound again. What if Jake Ritter had heard of his name and knew that he rode on the side of the law? He swallowed hard and decided to try his luck.

'Hayes,' he replied. 'Folks just call me Hayes.'

'Nope. I ain't heard of you,' Ritter said. 'But then, I don't get much time to read newspapers. Are you any good with that hunk of iron?'

'Reasonable.'

To the total surprise of Hayes, Jake Ritter holstered his gun and moved back to the door. He turned its handle, opened it a few inches and stared out into the darkness.

'What do you reckon is going on in this town, Hayes?'

Hayes was taken back by the question.

'Don't you know?'

'Nope.' Ritter glanced at the taller man. 'I ain't got the foggiest idea. I was hoping that maybe you knew.'

THREE

El Paso was bathed in the glowing light of a myriad street lanterns. This was the one Texan town which refused to acknowledge that fun ceased just because the sun had set. The noise from its countless saloons and other pleasure parlours all flowed out on to its wide streets, mingling until nothing could be heard except a continuous drumming sound. It was as if every heartbeat within El Paso had become one.

They were forged together in the mutual pursuit of having as much fun as possible whilst the money lasted.

All heartbeats with the exception of that of the elderly banker, Rufas McCabe.

His heart tolled to a different knell.

The El Paso Bank had locked its doors more than eight hours earlier, but he still sat in his unlit office, brooding. There seemed little point any longer in his walking the three blocks to his magnificent home. A home that was devoid of life and filled only with tortuous memories.

The man had not set foot out of the large stone building for nearly a week now. He just waited.

The light that splashed in through his stained-glass office window illuminated the sombre scene. The once pristine office was now littered with papers and trash that he had refused to allow anyone to touch during his long vigil. Trays of food remained untouched, for McCabe had no appetite for anything except news of his missing son.

This was a man with a broken heart.

Thirty-six years in the banking business had made the rotund McCabe far wealthier than he would ever admit, and yet it now seemed to the silent figure that it had all been for nothing.

The only thing he had ever truly treasured had been taken from him, making a mockery of his own existence.

He had been blessed with only one child in his brief marriage before his sickly spouse had succumbed to the fever which had swept across the Lone Star state fifteen years earlier.

But McCabe had not allowed his grief to ruin the relationship he had cherished with the son he had named Joseph. He had given the boy the best of everything and ensured that he grew to be honest and true. A son whom any man would have been proud to call his own.

Then one windswept day, only a matter of weeks earlier, the world of Rufas McCabe had come crashing down around him.

Whoever it was who had so expertly managed to kidnap Joseph had known everything there was to know about the young man and his habitual routine.

They had known where and how to strike. So efficiently that not one person within the large sprawling town had noticed anything out of the ordinary.

Joseph McCabe had simply disappeared off the face of the earth. There were no clues as to who had perpetrated this unholy deed and, at first, no obvious reason as to why anyone would have do so.

But the motive had arrived in the mail the following day.

McCabe sat in his office staring at the handwritten note in his hand. He could no longer see the writing because of the darkness that filled the room, but it mattered little. He knew every single word that was carefully marked out in pencil upon its now creased surface.

The banker had them carved into his soul.

The letter had demanded a ransom.

It listed the exact place where the ransom money had to be left. It even instructed the banker at what time the money had to be left and warned of what might happen to his precious offspring if he were to deviate from the instructions.

Rufas McCabe had followed them to the letter and yet his son had not been returned to him. He had pleaded with the sheriff to help try and locate his son, but the elected law had not managed to find any trace of Joseph, the abductors, or the ransom.

McCabe knew that there were many in El Paso who would not lift a finger to help a man who had as much wealth as he. He wondered if the sheriff had even tried to find his son at all.

Then, when he was in the depths of despair, McCabe had been told by one of the town's deputies that he ought to hire ex-lawman Cal Hayes. The deputy had said that if anyone could track the kidnappers down and have any hope of rescuing Joseph, it was Hayes.

Desperation had driven McCabe to Hayes's hotel door. He had given the young gunfighter $1000 and promised twice as much again if he managed to bring back his beloved son alive.

The banker knew that this was the last roll of his dice. If someone of Hayes's reputation could not achieve his goal, then no one else could either.

McCabe sat upright in his chair and rested the scrap of paper on top of his ink-blotter. Everything he cherished was now in the skilled hands of a man whom he had only met once. But what if the kidnappers had already killed Joseph?

Even Cal Hayes could not resurrect the dead.

The banker reached across his wide desk, lifted the whiskey bottle and tilted its neck until his glass was filled once more.

He downed the liquor swiftly and then rested his back against the soft padded leather of the seat. His eyes closed as the warmth of the drink burned its way down into his belly.

The bottle had been full when he had first lowered his ample frame into his large chair. Now there was less than a third left in the clear glass bottle.

But he was still sober.

It was as if no amount of liquor could blot out the thoughts that tortured him. He wanted to sleep but knew that there was no escape there either. For his every dream became a nightmare when the reality of his torment filtered into his slumbers. The banker cursed himself for being so old. So old that he could do nothing except wait.

He had always made his own way in life and yet now his entire future rested in the hands of a man whom he hardly knew.

McCabe had heard many men tell of how you could instinctively know when someone close to you was dead. They had all said the same thing, you just knew. It was like having a knife thrust into your heart.

A tear rolled down his left cheek and dripped on to an already damp jacket lapel.

However much Rufas McCabe tried to ignore the feeling, he could feel that knife in his aching, broken heart.

FOUR

Cal Hayes could not take his eyes off the imposing figure before him. It still seemed impossible that he was in the presence of the notorious Jake Ritter. A man whom he knew to be more dangerous than a sackful of rattlers.

Ritter closed the door again, then turned to face the gunfighter.

'You mean to tell me that you thought I had something to do with this town locking themselves away?' he asked.

'Yep. I have to admit the thought did mosey across my mind, Jake,' Hayes admitted.

Ritter shook his head and pointed to a pair of chairs at a table. Both men sat down on opposite sides of the table and continued eyeing one another cautiously.

'I rode in here about an hour before you

showed up,' Ritter said, pulling an expensive gold cigar-case from his inside jacket pocket. He pulled off its engraved lid. It contained three fat Havanas. 'Want one?'

Hayes shook his head.

'I never did master the art of smoking anything without coughing, Jake,' Hayes replied.

Ritter pulled one of the cigars out, then bit off its end and placed the object between his teeth. He returned the case to his pocket.

'Takes a real man to own up to his shortcomings, Hayes. I admire that.' The outlaw sighed.

Cal Hayes smiled as he watched the outlaw lean over the candle and suck in the smoke.

'Why did you stay here if you thought that something was wrong, Jake? I'd have thought that someone as skilled at his profession as you are would have ridden on out. After all, we ain't got no idea what them critters are doing behind them shutters.'

'I'm waiting for the rest of my gang to show up,' Ritter said through a cloud of smoke. 'I'm kinda stuck. It could be a trap but I doubt that. Nobody knew that me or my boys were heading here.'

Hayes nodded.

'Does put you in a awkward position and no mistake.'

'Damn right. I told Frank and the rest of the gang to meet with me here and them boys ain't the brightest lanterns in the street, if you catch my drift?'

'You mean, if they show up and you ain't here, they'll get a tad confused?' Hayes leaned back in his chair and winced. He suddenly knew where every bruise from the outlaw's pistol barrel was on his wide back.

'Damn right.' Ritter blew out a long line of smoke and narrowed his eyes. 'I have to lead them boys around by their damn noses sometimes. Frank ain't much brighter than the rest of the gang.'

The gunfighter watched as the brooding outlaw ran a thumb down his jawline and glanced at the door thoughtfully.

'What's wrong, Jake?'

'Why the hell would an entire town lock themselves away like that, Hayes? It don't make any sense.'

Hayes's mind began to race. Ritter was as much in the dark about why this town was all boarded up as he was himself. He felt sweat trickling down his face.

'I got me the impression as I was riding in, that they don't want certain folks to spot this little town,' Hayes said. 'I can't think of another reason for them to keep all the street lights extinguished.'

Ritter agreed. 'Yeah, there must be someone that they are trying to fool into thinking that they've hightailed it out of here.'

'That's why they hid the horses.'

'Exactly.'

Cal Hayes pushed the brim of his hat up and stared at the outlaw. For the first time since he had accidentally bumped into Ritter, Hayes felt as if he could let him know why he was here himself.

'I'm here to find the kidnapped son of an El Paso banker, Jake.'

Ritter tapped the cigar and watched the white ash fall to the dirt floor. There was little expression on his face as his eyes flashed at him.

'I thought you said that you was a gunfighter?'

'I am. This job just fell into my lap and the banker offered me too much money for me to refuse.' Hayes knew that the man across the table from him lived his life by never allowing himself to trust anyone. That was why he was still alive when so many of his fellow outlaws had long since met their Maker.

'Was the boy kidnapped?' Ritter seemed far more interested than Hayes had imagined he would be.

'Yep. Some varmints managed to snatch the youngster right from under the nose of everyone in El Paso.'

'You followed their trail here?' Ritter placed the cigar between his teeth and looked along its length at Hayes.

'Yep. Nobody else seemed to be able to

find a trail, but I guess I got lucky.'

'I got a kid.' Ritter said thoughtfully. 'I'd kill anyone who tried to hurt that child.'

Hayes was surprised by the statement. He suddenly saw that for all the killings that this man had probably been involved in, he was still a father. He did have some feelings remaining inside his otherwise deadly soul.

'I ain't never found me a woman who'd sit still long enough for me to get serious, Jake.'

'Maybe that makes you luckier than me.' The outlaw looked sad as he stared at the blue smoke rising up from the end of his Havana. 'A man gets hurt whenever he allows his feeling for others to show.'

'Reckon so.'

Ritter removed the cigar from his thin lips and rested his elbows on the table. His icy stare had a way of glueing a man to his seat. The gunfighter felt the power of the legendary outlaw keeping him exactly where he wanted him. It was like an invisible force that only a fool would ignore.

'So you managed to track them bastards

here?' Ritter's voice was low and serious. 'All the way from El Paso.'

Hayes nodded.

'Yep.'

'How many men are you tracking?'

'I reckon there are six riders all told. I've managed to detect at least six different sets of horseshoe tracks. One of them has to be the banker's son.' Cal Hayes had watched the outlaw's head moving up and down as he listened intently to the words which fell from his own dry lips.

'Are you sure that one of the riders is the banker's son?' The question came at the gunfighter fast. 'How do you know that they ain't already killed the kid?'

'I spent half the first day scouting out every trail in and out of El Paso, Jake,' Hayes replied. 'If they had killed the lad, my nostrils would have led me straight to the corpse. He's alive, OK.'

The outlaw stood and looked at the door again, then returned his attention to his seated companion.

'Why would they keep him alive?'

'That I have yet to figure, Jake.'

'It don't make sense to haul around a prisoner when there ain't no profit in it.' Ritter seemed to hear his own words and then correct himself. 'Unless they have a bigger, more profitable plan already worked out. One that requires the kid remain alive.'

'What kinda plan?' Hayes knew that if anyone could work out the way outlaws thought, it was Jake Ritter.

There was a long silence. Ritter just stood motionless thinking of every trick that the kidnappers might employ to milk even more money out of the El Paso banker. Then he tapped his chin with his index finger.

'Do you have any objection to my helping you try and find that kid, Hayes?' Ritter asked.

Hayes rose to his feet. Once again the outlaw had taken him by surprise.

'Nope, but I ought to tell you that the banker's son is eighteen. He ain't no little boy.'

Ritter placed the cigar back in his mouth and then pulled out a pair of black kid gloves. He put them on his small hands. He tugged at the fingers in turn until the gloves were so tight, they felt and looked like a second skin.

'Don't matter none to me how old he is.' Ritter sighed.

'I didn't want you to get the idea that I was trying to mislead you, Jake.' Hayes swallowed hard.

'He's still someone's son and he don't deserve to be taken from his father like that.' Ritter moved to the door and gripped the handle again. He opened it a few inches and stared into the darkness. 'And his pa don't deserve to worry about his boy, even if he is a banker.'

'You serious about helping me round up these critters?'

'Damn serious, Hayes.' Jake Ritter almost allowed his face to smile. 'Frank and the boys are always keeping me waiting, so maybe I'll keep them waiting for a change if we have to take us a ride following them bastard kidnappers. Besides, it'll do the gang good to worry about me.'

'I'm sure happy that you're on my side, Jake.'

Ritter continued looking out into the dark streets.

'But first we ought to find out why all the folks in this town are hiding behind shuttered doors.'

Hayes stepped to the side of the outlaw and placed a hand on the man's arm. Each man looked into the other's eyes.

'What if it's the men I'm seeking who are behind those shuttered doors, Jake?'

'Then we'll kill them, Hayes.' Jake Ritter walked out into the darkness with the gun-fighter on his heels. 'We'll kill them good.'

FIVE

Gunfighter Cal Hayes stayed close to Jake Ritter as they slowly made their way through the silent streets and alleys that made up the maze of wooden buildings which surrounded them. The town was bathed in darkness and there were far too many shadows for them safely to split up in their search for the people they knew were here.

At first they simply walked shoulder to shoulder along the soft sandy streets, waiting for a clue as to which of the buildings were occupied.

Then Ritter stopped walking and pointed the barrel of his cocked and readied Schofield at a small building set between a feed-store and a barbershop.

Hayes bit his lower lip and squinted at the structure. Whatever had caught the outlaw's eye was not evident to him.

'What you see, Jake?'

Ritter removed the cigar from his mouth and dropped it on to the sand. He crushed it with his right boot.

'Someone's in there for sure, Hayes.'

'You certain?'

'Damn right!' Ritter walked up to the front of the narrow wooden building and studied the locked door before him. He then glanced up at two small windows above their heads.

'What did you see?' Hayes asked, gripping his Peacemaker firmly in his sweating hand.

'A candle upstairs. Somebody blew it out when they saw us in the street,' Ritter answered. He turned the door handle.

'Locked?'

'Not for long, Hayes.' Ritter raised the barrel of his Smith & Wesson, trained it on the lock of the door and then squeezed the trigger. The single shot was deafening amid the total silence that surrounded them both. The brass lock shattered into countless fragments leaving a large hole in the door.

Jake Ritter poked the barrel of his pistol into what was left of the lock and rotated it. Small pieces of metal fell into the building before the outlaw extracted the gun. The door creaked as it was pushed open.

'C'mon, Hayes!' Ritter said before rushing inside. 'Let's take us a look at who's in this place.'

Cal Hayes followed. Both men had their guns raised in readiness for action. Ritter satisfied himself that there was no one on the ground floor before moving to the foot of the staircase and peering up into the darkness.

Both men aimed their weapons at what they took to be the top of the stairs and then started to walk slowly up the bare boards.

Again, they were shoulder to shoulder.

Like a pair of well-armed bookends. Ready for whatever might jump out before their cocked pistols.

Suddenly a noise from above them stopped the pair in their tracks. Ritter's honed in-stincts made him step ahead of his companion and aim his gun in the direction of the noise.

'Don't shoot!' a terrified voice screamed out.

Hayes rested his left hand on Ritter's forearm.

'That was a woman, Jake.'

Ritter glanced at the gunfighter. Somehow the whites of his eyes sparkled at the man a step below him.

'I know a female when I hear one, Hayes. I ain't that out of touch.'

'Who are you?' Her voice was young. Maybe twenty or a little older. 'Please don't hurt us. Please, I beg you. Don't hurt us.'

A cold chill ran down the spines of both the armed men. They had never expected to hear such a pitiful plea and it made them uncomfortable.

'Take it easy, ma'am,' Hayes called out. 'We ain't gonna harm nobody unless they try to hurt us first.'

'Who are you?' the female called out again.

'The name's Hayes and this is...'

The outlaw pressed his black gloved left hand over Hayes's mouth. Both men looked at one another and suddenly knew that it would not help their cause if they told her that the notorious Jake Ritter was heading up towards her.

'And this is my partner,' Hayes called up to the frightened female.

'The name's Jake, ma'am,' Ritter added.

They could see movement in the depths of the black shadows above them. Neither man could make out who or what was now standing directly at the top of the flight of wooden steps.

'Is that you, ma'am?' Cal Hayes asked cautiously watching for any sign of trouble.

'Yes. I'm alone here.' Her voice was now steady and yet neither man trusted her. She sounded too confident. They had both learned the hard way long ago that even the sweetest of voices could be deadly.

'Can we come up?' Ritter gripped his pistol at his side. He was ready to use it if necessary.

There was a long pause before she spoke again.

'You may.'

Jake Ritter continued to ascend the stairs once more, with Hayes keeping only one step below him. The closer the two men got, the clearer the female became. The outlaw stared at her wide skirt which he knew had at least six layers of petticoats padding it out. There was plenty of room behind that skirt for a gunman to hide, he thought.

He'd found them in less likely places.

Both men stopped at the top of the staircase and looked hard at her. She did not flinch.

Even the shadows could not disguise her beauty from their weary eyes. She looked scared and yet stubborn. Her long wavy hair cascaded on to her narrow shoulders in a way that men noticed.

'What do you want here?' she asked.

Hayes eased past Ritter and removed his hat.

'Don't be afraid, ma'am. We are just two

men on the trail of some kidnappers.'

Her head tilted back. 'I'm not afraid of either of you.'

Ritter smiled.

'You got spirit, young lady. A whole barrel of it.'

Cal Hayes cleared his throat nervously. He had never met anyone quite so small with as much grit as she displayed.

'Can you tell us what's going on in this town, ma'am?'

'Stop calling me ma'am, my name's Rose Duggan.'

'Rose is a nice name,' Hayes said.

'Careful, Hayes,' Ritter warned. 'Roses have got thorns.'

She looked defiant.

'Why should I tell you drifters anything?'

Jake Ritter stepped up on to the landing and moved to a window behind her. He pulled the drapes apart and looked down into the street below them. His eyes had adjusted to the darkness and he was able to make out the outline of the buildings below him.

'Careful, Hayes. She's getting rough.'

The female allowed Hayes to step a little closer before planting her knuckles on her hips and glaring up at him.

'Well? Why should I tell you? Are you the law?'

Ritter gave a muffled chuckle.

'I don't rightly know why you should tell us anything, but it might help us understand a few things,' Hayes told her.

Ritter continued looking out of the window as he spoke in his turn:

'Something is going on in this town, Rose. Something that don't sit well with us. It'd be a kindness if you could tell us why the entire town seems to be hiding away behind locked doors.'

She lowered her hands.

'What's left of the townsfolk you mean,' she said.

Ritter allowed the lace drape to fall back into place and was about to speak again when the windowpane beside him shattered into a million fragments. The sound of a gun being fired down in the street echoed around the wooden buildings as the outlaw swung around on his heels in pain.

Hayes pulled the girl aside and rushed to the side of his companion. He pushed him up against the wall.

'You OK?'

Jake Ritter checked his right shoulder with the fingers of his left hand. He could feel a burning pain on the top of his left bicep.

'It's just a flesh wound, Hayes,' the outlaw snarled, pushing his way past the taller man and moving the lace drape with the barrel of his Schofield. Another bullet blasted through the window. Ritter felt the heat of it on his face as it passed within inches of his head.

'C'mon. Let's try and get them,' Hayes said. He ran across the landing and dashed down the wooden staircase.

Ritter cocked the hammer of his gun and fired.

Another bullet hit the window.

'I'm starting to get a mite angry,' Ritter

muttered before following the gunfighter down the staircase and out into the street.

Both men stood with their guns raised. Ritter walked to the gunfighter's side and indicated for him to follow. Hayes did.

The pair moved through the shadows into the nearest alley, then headed in the direction that they both knew would take them to the rear of the small house. A tall seven-foot-high fence hid their advance from view.

Suddenly another shot was fired. Ritter raised his left hand and pressed his gloved hand against Hayes's chest, stopping him in his tracks.

The gunfighter bit his lower lip and watched the outlaw edging his way to the corner of the fence.

'You shooting at me, mister?' Jake Ritter asked the man standing in the dark alley. The man swung around and fired at the same time that Ritter fanned the hammer of his gun three times.

Hayes rushed forward and stared at the sight of the man lying less than twelve feet from the outlaw.

'You got him!'

Ritter emptied the spent shells from his gun and quickly reloaded.

'Of course I did. I'm Jake Ritter.'

SIX

For more than five hours the riders had been slowly making their way up the treacherous trail which led up and over the high tree-covered mountainside. This was not a route that any rider would have taken unless driven by desperation. Its soft crumbling trail was dangerous even in daylight, but at night, with no moon to guide them, it was perilous indeed. They had left the valley far below them as they tried vainly to shake off their pursuers.

But it seemed to the fleeing horsemen who gazed down at the flickering torches that there was no way that the men who followed could be so easily fooled.

It was as if the man-hunters had the ability to anticipate every move of their prey.

Outlaw Frank Ritter and the rest of his gang were behind schedule in reaching the remote town where they knew Jake would already be waiting, but there was no way he would deliberately lead whoever it was behind them to his younger brother.

The seven exhausted riders had been trying to shake off the posse that had somehow tagged on to their trail more than a week earlier, but it had become evident that, whoever they were, they were no ordinary bunch.

It seemed to the wily Frank Ritter that the twenty or so horsemen who doggedly followed them had to be a hand-picked crew of hunters. He had noticed before the sun had set that the lead rider rode a dapple-grey pony. The outlaw had heard tell of a tame Crow Indian scout called Walking Horse Man who was reputed to be able to track men through rivers and hard rock. Nobody had ever managed to escape from his keen tracking skills.

Walking Horse Man rode a dapple-grey.

Frank Ritter had not mentioned this to any of the six men who steered their mounts along the narrow trail up the side of the tree covered mountain. The last thing he wanted was for any of the outlaws behind him to panic. This was no place to get skittish.

Frank doubted that his cousins, Colt, Lee and Jim Yancy would allow their imaginations to run riot. They had been through too many battles together for a mere posse to trouble them. It was the new men he had hired to replace those lost during their last train robbery who worried him.

Sam Liddle, Tom Parker and Jock Johnson were all young and untested. All of the loud-voiced outlaws talked big, but Frank had his doubts whether they were as experienced or good under pressure as they claimed. He had been told by Jake to hire three new men, and that was what he had done. It seemed that all the seasoned outlaws had disappeared one way or another. Those who were left would never have even been considered a few years earlier.

But the pickings were slim and beggars could not be choosers.

The black roan, with its long white legs, felt its master pull back on its reins. This magnificent mount was one of only two such animals in the territories. The other belonged to Jake Ritter. Frank hauled in his reins, rested his gloved right wrist on the saddle horn and stood in his stirrups.

He had only one thought. Was the posse still on their trail?

Reluctantly, the outlaw had to acknowledge that it was.

Frank Ritter screwed up his eyes and gazed down into the tree-filled canyon below their high vantage point and then spat at the ground.

The scout, with a torch in his left hand, had started up the narrow mountain trail with the rest of the posse in single file behind his dapple-grey.

'Damn! Ain't they ever gonna quit?' he growled.

'They just have to be Pinkerton men, Frank,' Colt Yancy said as he stroked the neck of his tired mount. 'We must have pushed the railroad companies just about as far as we can. They're fighting back.'

'Whoever they are, they ain't ordinary riders.' Frank searched in his pocket, pulled out a block of tobacco and bit off a massive chunk. He started to chew vigorously. He knew that there was no way that he could lead these lawmen to his brother.

'We have to get over this mountain and get to Jake. He'll know what to do,' Jim Yancy suggested.

'We gotta shake off this pack of wolves first, Jim,' a stern Frank said, as brown spittle trickled down from the corner of his mouth. 'I ain't leading them to Jake. That's what they want us to do.'

Colt nodded and looked back at the faces of the men behind them.

'Frank's right. We have to get away from

these bastards before we head on to meet up with Jake.'

There was a groan along the line of horsemen. They'd ridden around in circles for days trying to confuse the men who hunted them, but so far, they hadn't been able to shake them off. These were no ordinary riders.

'I thought that you said we were heading to Jake?' Jock Johnson grumbled. 'I ain't gonna ride around these mountains for the rest of my life.'

Lee Yancy turned in his saddle and pointed a finger at the new men.

'Hush up. If you ride with us, you do as we say. You ain't got no vote in what Frank decided.'

Sam Liddle shrugged. 'I knew that you was old, but I thought ya still had some guts.'

Frank glanced at the six men behind him. Their faces were as troubled as his own. They had not been able to stop and rest for days now and every one of them was sore and angry.

'We're all tired, Sam. But that posse has to

be as tuckered out as we are.'

Frank had to try and keep his entire gang sweet if they were to survive until dawn. Three of his gang he knew he could trust with his life. He had done so for years. They would follow wherever he led them because they were kin.

He had to try and give the three new men a chance to prove themselves, but Frank did not know whether they would prove a help or liability.

He had yet to test them in battle. That was where he would be able to gauge their worth, in the heat of battle.

'What we gonna do, Frank?' Colt Yancy asked. He placed his unlit pipe between his teeth.

Frank spat out a large black lump of goo and then rubbed his chin on the back of his sleeve. They were in a situation that he had not anticipated and had little understanding of. For all his years as a soldier and robber, he had never been hunted before.

'Reckon we ain't got much choice in the

'matter,' Frank said thoughtfully.

'We gonna fight?' Tom Parker piped up.

Sam Liddle began to chuckle almost childishly. 'We gonna pick the bastards off with our Winchesters?'

'Eventually we'll do both them things, boys.' Frank gathered up his reins in his gloved hands and then tapped his spurs into the flesh of his lathered-up mount. 'But not here. We have to find us a place where the cover is better. We ain't gonna stand up to twenty men with repeating rifles with our seven. We have to have the advantage on them *hombres*. If we start shooting up here our horses will spook and lose their footing. They'll take us down into the abyss faster than the Devil has time to prepare a reception party for us in purgatory.'

A silence gathered over the three new riders. This was far more serious than any of them had at first realized. When you rode with the Ritter and Yancy boys, you rode with men.

'I don't like it. They just keep on coming.

How?' Johnson asked fretfully.

Frank glanced down into the valley and the sight of the torches that three of the horsemen were carrying. They were now starting to climb the same trail that he and his gang had travelled up hours earlier.

They were getting closer with every beat of his heart.

'Come on. We have to find a better place. A place where we can kill without being killed,' Frank said, holding on to his reins tightly. 'This sure ain't it.'

The six outlaws followed the elder Ritter brother higher into the tall trees.

SEVEN

The arrival of dawn offered Hayes and Ritter few clues as to what exactly was happening in the quiet town. Apart from finding the dead outlaw's horse tied up out of sight behind the livery stable, they were none the wiser. They returned to the alley behind the small house and the body that still lay where it had fallen with three of Jake Ritter's well placed bullets in it.

Cal Hayes stood and watched whilst Ritter knelt down to study his handiwork. The outlaw rolled the now stiff body over and looked at the neat grouping of holes in the centre of the man's chequered shirt. The blood had long since dried as the black-gloved hands ripped the shirt apart.

Ritter stared at the holes in the hairy chest of the man.

'Not bad, considering I couldn't even see the back-shooting bastard. Huh, Hayes?'

Hayes stepped closer and watched as his companion inspected the body and the clothes he was wearing.

'What ya looking for, Jake?'

Ritter did not reply. His fingers kept turning out each of the dead man's pockets. It was as if he was searching for something, but Hayes could not imagine what. The gloved hand pulled out a small bag filled with sparkling golden eagles.

'Fresh minted,' Ritter said before sliding the bag into his jacket pocket and resuming his search. 'I figure that was his share of the ransom money.'

Hayes leaned further over the body.

'You could be right. He might be one of the riders I've been trailing.'

Then Ritter paused.

'Damn,' he muttered, lifting the stiff arm.

'What is it?' Hayes asked.

Ritter pointed at the man's left hand. It was a hand that only had a thumb and ring-finger.

'You know who this is, Hayes?' Ritter asked.

'Nope. I ain't never set eyes on him before,' came the honest reply. 'Who is he?'

'This is Two Fingers Jones!' The outlaw grinned.

Hayes was none the wiser although he knew that the name should mean something to him.

'Who is he?'

'A back-stabbing purse-thief from Dodge,' Ritter stated. 'The sort that likes to rob old ladies. The last time I heard of this critter he was riding with Big Bill O'Mara.'

Hayes was still no wiser.

'I never heard of either of them.'

Ritter dropped the arm.

'This little man is worth five hundred dollars dead. Kinda makes me wish I was a bounty hunter. Sad to see that money going to waste.'

Cal Hayes looked up and noticed Rose Duggan watching them from the shot-out window of her house. He felt uneasy. He and Ritter had entered a dozen of the stores and houses in the town and yet had not found another living soul in any of the buildings that they had searched. But that did not mean that every house was empty.

He tilted his head back and stared up at her. She had her knuckles on her hips. Hayes began to wonder why she had remained in the town when it appeared that every other person had fled. Or perhaps they had not run away.

A cold shudder traced the gunfighter's spine. He glanced around them at the sandy streets and the fertile fields that lay beyond the wooden buildings.

What if some ruthless gang of killers had murdered every one of the townsfolk and buried their bodies far away from prying eyes? His eyes darted back to the window but Rose Duggan was gone.

Perhaps she was the only survivor?

'I figure that he's one of the men you've been tracking, Hayes,' Ritter said confidently.

'That's all very interesting, Jake,' Cal Hayes answered, rubbing his chin. 'But it don't explain where the rest of the townsfolk have gone, does it?'

The outlaw stood up. He had something in his hands which he was staring at.

'Don't it?'

Hayes's full attention returned to the man beside him. He stepped over the body and went to stand beside Ritter.

'What you got there?'

The outlaw showed the gunfighter the scrap of paper he had discovered in the inside jacket pocket of Two Fingers Jones.

'I reckon that this might answer a few of them damn questions, Hayes.'

Cal Hayes accepted the paper and looked at it hard. The pencil marks were crude, written by someone who had little knowledge of the English language or spelling. But someone who did, however, need to make notes in case he forgot vital details.

'This explains a lot,' Hayes said quietly.

'It sure does,' Ritter agreed. 'It tells us why most of the folks around here cleared out. It also gives us a clue as to where that banker's son has been taken.'

'Big Bill's men must have frightened these folks off,' Hayes said softly. 'Except maybe a couple who are too stubborn to be scared off by anyone.'

'Like the thorny Rose?'

'Yep.'

'I figure that Big Bill knew that they were

being trailed and he left Two Fingers here to bushwhack whoever showed up.'

Ritter nodded.

'Then how come he didn't take a shot at you when you rode in?' Hayes continued, looking at the paper as he spoke. 'And he didn't shoot at me either, come to think of it.'

The outlaw paced up and down in the alley and mumbled to himself for nearly a minute. Then he snapped the fingers of his gloved right hand and moved back to the side of the gunfighter.

'Maybe old Two Fingers got himself a little drunk and was sleeping until I shot off the doorhandle to Rose Duggan's house.' Jake Ritter nodded again. He instinctively knew that had to be the answer. 'The sound of the shot woke the critter up from his drunken stupor. Then he come looking for us.'

'You sure he was drinking, Jake?'

Ritter pointed at the body. 'His body still stinks of whiskey and he's been dead for hours.'

'That makes sense.' Hayes nodded. 'The

back door of the saloon in the main street had been forced open.'

'Damn right, Hayes.'

Cal Hayes walked beside the outlaw along the alley. It looked different in the light of day. The danger had evaporated into the heat haze that rose off the sun-baked ground. Both men were making their way to the house where they had left the female a couple of hours earlier, before they had set out after Jones.

'Who is this Big Bill character?' the gunfighter asked as they stepped up on to the boardwalk outside the barbershop.

'A low-life,' Ritter replied. 'I reckon he must be behind the kidnapping. Two Fingers was one of the scum who rode with him and did his bidding.'

'Is he dangerous?'

'Like a bag full of sidewinders.'

'According to the note, Two Fingers was to meet up with Big Bill and the rest of his gang at a place I've never heard of before.' Hayes stared at the crude drawing on the paper beside the writing. 'What does this mean, Jake?'

Both men paused by the door of the house where they had discovered Rose Duggan. Ritter looked hard at the drawing.

'It looks like a bird to me.'

Hayes rubbed his chin again.

'You ever heard of a place that has anything to do with a bird, Jake?'

The outlaw's eyes brightened.

'Eagle's Rock!' he exclaimed.

'Where is that?'

Ritter saw the figure of Rose Duggan descending the stairs, coming towards them. He looked at his companion's face. Cal Hayes could not take his eyes off her.

'It's about twenty miles west from here.'

At last the gunfighter turned his attention to the outlaw.

'You want to take a ride, Jake?'

'Damn right!'

EIGHT

The face of Pinkerton agent Dan Larrigan was the epitome of the law itself. A hard unyielding face that bore the scars of a lifetime's upholding of the values of a system that he no longer understood or questioned.

Nearly fifty years old and over six feet in height, the rider from Kentucky had all the physical attributes that made men listen when he spoke. Yet of late he seemed to speak less and less.

The older he got the more he seemed to withdraw into his own company. Some thought that it was a sign of his inner strength, which allowed him to lead his fellow detectives without ever having to raise his voice.

Others knew the truth.

Larrigan had become hardened to the job

he had excelled at since joining the élite Pinkerton force. He no longer tried to work out whether the men he sought were guilty of the crimes that they were accused of. There was no time for that in the new age of crime fighting.

He just followed orders blindly, without emotion.

When given the task of locating the Ritter–Yancy gang by his superiors back East, Larrigan recruited all available agents from over five states and set to work.

This was the biggest case he had ever been assigned to, and he was determined it would not get the better of him. He cared little for the reputations of those he hunted. For there had not been anyone born in the last half-century whom he feared.

There were no borders when you worked for Pinkerton. You just carried out the job in hand with a cold detachment that put fear into the hearts of all who stood in your way. It seemed that there were no lawmen anywhere who would stand up against the renowned agency and its operatives.

The Pinkerton men were a law unto themselves.

Yet not all who had been recruited by the famous 'seeing eye' detective agency were as honest as Larrigan. Most were no better than the human prey they hunted.

Some were far worse.

So it was with the riders who followed the determined Dan Larrigan as they slowly trailed Frank Ritter and his gang up the steep mountainside. A few were true to the oath that they had sworn in order to become Pinkerton men, but the majority of horsemen were little better than bandits and thieves themselves.

For several years Larrigan had tried to sift out the vermin whom he was forced to employ, but to no avail. For once a man had been signed on as a Pinkerton detective, there was nothing that could strip him of his badge or credentials.

It seemed that however respected their illustrious leader was, he cared little for the morals he professed in his advertising literature.

For the Pinkerton men were hired by the most powerful individuals in America. They travelled with presidents and were answerable to no one except Pinkerton himself.

And Allan Pinkerton asked no questions.

The reams of stories and reports of cruelty, murder and depravity that men like Larrigan sent to their superiors back East were simply dismissed.

It was impossible for there to be any rogue agents in such a famous institution as the one created by Allan Pinkerton.

Larrigan knew it was pointless to continue his crusade. He had given up doing anything except following orders.

That was why the tall rider from Kentucky had become hardened to his vocation. He had decided it was useless even trying to point an accusing finger at any of the less honest members of the agency.

No one cared.

Larrigan just continued silently spurring

his mount on up through the trees after the dapple-grey of the skilled Crow scout called Walking Horse Man.

The eighteen mounted agents who followed in single file were a mixed bunch, as usual, but Larrigan knew that if they did manage to close the gap between themselves and the Ritter–Yancy outfit, they would be tested.

There was no room here on this perilous mountain trail for corruption.

Only courage and gun skills would determine who was the victor when the fighting started. Perhaps it would take the bullets of outlaws to filter out the rotten apples from the Pinkerton barrel, he thought.

The Kentucky rider with the weathered face smiled knowingly. You could not bribe or cheat your way out of a fight with men like Frank and Jake Ritter.

Bad as they undoubtedly were, they fought and were prepared to die like men.

NINE

It was an ominous place by anyone's standards. A place where no man visited through choice. This was somewhere that men only rode to when driven by necessity. Yet it served as a refuge for those who needed to hide from the prying eyes of their betters.

Eagle's Rock was aptly named. The peak of a bald mountain top had been carved by nature itself over countless generations until it actually resembled the head of a proud bald eagle.

But it was not the rocky summit that men sought out for sanctuary, it was the massive caves at the base of the tree-covered mountain, which they knew offered them unparalleled protection from those wanting to claim the rewards on their heads.

For more than a dozen years outlaws had

used the large caves to hide from all who tried to find them.

A solitary rocky trail led over the high mountain less than a quarter-mile from the unseen caves. Apart from the occasional Indian hunting party, no one else ventured within a hundred miles of the remote trail.

But the heavily forested mountain had its own dangers lurking for the unwary. Bears and mountain lions freely roamed this terrain and would claim anyone who crossed their trails. But compared to having their necks stretched by a hangman's rope, the outlaws who hid at Eagle's Rock felt no fear of its ferocious creatures.

Eagle's Rock was one of the few places in the untamed territory which the badmen knew they could rely upon to protect them.

Few honest men had any knowledge at all of the existence of the caves.

But the men who crouched beneath the granite overhang were far from honest. They were of a different breed. A breed that has plagued good folks since time itself began.

Big Bill O'Mara was, as his name suggested, big.

Yet his size was dwarfed by the evil that flowed through his veins instead of blood. Nothing was beyond this creature in human form and all who had ever encountered him knew it.

For long ago O'Mara had learned every trick in the book of how to steal, rape and kill without giving a damn for his victims.

His sort were rare even in the bowels of Hell.

And that was where it was rumoured he had been spawned.

He crouched and gazed out at the view before him. To him the million trees were his army. They would protect him from anyone who tried to get close to his hideout.

The wild animals which moved unseen between those tree trunks were his infantry.

Big Bill O'Mara continued crouching and staring out at the impenetrable green canopy below him as his men prepared the caves for their brief stay.

He had already worked out the next part of his despicable plan and would wait exactly six days before returning to the distant El Paso to put it into action.

O'Mara knew that Rufas McCabe still had a lot more money in that fat juicy bank of his and would willingly part with every cent of it to buy the freedom of his son.

The outlaw began to chuckle.

It was the depraved laughter of the Devil himself.

TEN

Dan Larrigan kicked the dry dust over what was left of the small camp-fire perched high on the side of the perilous mountain trail and then looked at his men. They had eaten what was left of their rations and consumed at least one cup of coffee each since he had awoken them. Only the silent Crow scout had neither eaten or had anything to drink since waking.

The Indian just crouched beneath his blanket, holding on to his reins, staring up at what was left of the trail they still had to negotiate. The top of the mountain trail led to another valley and more tall straight trees.

Larrigan had decided the previous night that it was getting far too dangerous for them to continue following the Ritter–Yancy gang any further up the treacherous route, and had made camp. Yet the Pinkerton man had not managed to close his eyes for one minute of the four hours that he had allowed the posse to sleep.

He wondered whether the outlaws had also rested or had continued to flee the relentless pursuers whom he led. Larrigan then began to try and think what he would do in their position.

Walking Horse Man glanced at the men who all sported their gleaming badges on their vests. Yet of all of them, he only trusted the silent Dan Larrigan.

The quiet Indian knew that the riders whom he led were no better than the ones they were trailing. They had the smell of death on their long trail coats. A smell which told the Crow many things that they would never realize he knew.

His hooded eyes concealed a thousand thoughts, but he, like the rest of his kind, would never reveal any of them to white men.

Larrigan carefully walked past the seated posse until he was at the side of Walking Horse Man. He knelt and stared hard at the scout's expressionless face.

'Do you know this land?'

The Indian nodded. 'I know.'

Larrigan pulled out his tobacco pouch and started making a cigarette. The scout's hooded eyes watched the man's nimble fingers rolling the paper and then raising it to his tongue.

Walking Horse Man accepted the cigarette and placed it between his lips.

'Will we catch up with them today?' Larrigan asked. He struck a match on the rocky ground and lifted the flame to the end of the cigarette. He watched as the Crow inhaled deeply.

'There will be a big battle before this day is over.'

'You reckon we'll win?' Larrigan blew the flame out and tossed the match into the deep valley.

With smoke filtering through his teeth the Indian tilted his head back and stared up until he was staring straight into the blazing sun.

'There will be many dead before the sun sets, Larrigan.'

'But will we win?'

'There will be no winners,' Walking Horse Man declared. 'There will only be dead men littering the forest.'

Dan Larrigan stood and sighed heavily. He looked at the rest of his posse.

'Get up, boys. We'll walk the horses the rest of the way to the top of the trail.'

It did not take long for Cal Hayes's

experienced eyes to locate the trail left by the hoofs of the remaining five riders. It led due west from the small town. It was straight and true, like the flight path of an arrow that had been aimed at the distant mountain range where Jake Ritter said they would find Eagle's Rock.

It was obvious to the keen-eyed Hayes that Big Bill O'Mara had not even attempted to cover his trail to the remote outlaw hideout. He had assumed that his henchman, Two Fingers, would stop the gunfighter who followed them, permanently.

Hayes had not given much thought to taking supplies on the difficult journey that lay ahead. Jake Ritter, however, had. He had learned long ago the value of having adequate provisions when venturing into unknown territories.

Using the mount of the late Two Fingers Jones as a pack-horse, Hayes and Ritter had set out from the small isolated town just before noon. They had left the still-pouting Rose Duggan behind them, but not before learning a few things from her that could prove vital information when they met up with the men whom they sought.

Rose had told them that Big Bill O'Mara had visited the town several times before using it as a base from where he could reach out and strike at El Paso. But O'Mara was not the sort of man who could simply enter a town without trying to control it.

Rose had given Hayes and Ritter vivid details of the mindless atrocities O'Mara and his henchmen had inflicted on the men, women and even children who had once occupied the houses and businesses around her own home.

It had been so easy.

Big Bill O'Mara had killed the sheriff within hours of his first arrival and done far worse on his return visits. Apart from the defiant Rose, every other soul who had survived fled the town when news of O'Mara's impending return reached them.

They had suffered enough. There was no way they could stand any further pain. With their most valued possessions in tow, they fled into the dense brush.

Even Jake Ritter was surprised that an entire town could be so frightened of a handful of men that they would willingly flee their homes rather than face them again.

The two horsemen led the pack-horse across the knee-high swaying grass towards the dark forest.

'How far is it to Eagle's Rock, Jake?' Hayes asked. He teased the reins with his left hand as his right wrist rested on the grip of his holstered Colt Peacemaker.

'About twenty miles as the crow flies,' came the reply. Jake stared off into the distance before them.

'If it's only twenty miles, how come we can't see that eagle's head on the top of that mountain yet?' Hayes gestured with his left hand at the dense forest of trees before them.

Ritter turned his head and narrowed his eyes as he stared at his companion.

''Coz that ain't the mountain, Hayes.'

'It ain't?'

'Nope.' Ritter turned his head and continued looking straight ahead. 'The mountain with the eagle's head on top of it is the one beyond that one.'

Cal Hayes felt his heart sink.

'You mean we have to get over that mountain before we get to the mountain we're looking for?'

Jake Ritter laughed.

'Now ya starting to get to grips with the situation.'

'Damn.' Hayes sighed.

'Damn right, Hayes.' The outlaw laughed.

ELEVEN

The outlaws had not stopped during the long hours of darkness to rest themselves or their mounts. They knew that whoever it was on their trail might keep following them as they had done during the previous couple

87

of nights. There was no way that Frank Ritter could afford to run the risk of having twenty well-armed riders catch up with them whilst they were sleeping.

This was not a land in which you could relax for even a mere minute. This land favoured the hunter, not the hunted. Yet when the seven horsemen had reached the bottom of the steep mountainside and the sun rose to announce a new day, it had become clear that the posse must have stopped somewhere over the high ridge and made camp.

Knowing this, the cunning outlaw leader had then decided that their best plan was to try and lure the score of lawmen into a well-laid trap.

Frank Ritter tied his reins to a tall swaying sapling and gazed around at the faces of his gang. Their seven mounts were now in a deep gully, well away from the place where he had chosen to make a stand against the posse.

For day after day they had been unable to shake the Indian scout and his followers off their trail. Now Frank Ritter was determined to use that fact and turn it against them.

The posse seemed to be able to trail his gang however much care he and his men had taken to leave no tracks.

This would be their undoing.

Jim Yancy stood chewing on a tobacco plug silently watching the rest of the men around him. Of all his cousins, Frank knew that Jim was the most reliable. He never questioned anything or anyone.

He simply obeyed.

'Keep ya eye on the new men, Jim,' Frank said as he walked past him. 'I got me a bad feeling about them boys letting us down when the shooting starts.'

Jim spat and then nodded. He looked in the direction of Liddle, Parker and Johnson, then walked away from the line of horses. He pointed at them.

'C'mon, young 'uns. We got to get to our places before that damn posse comes over the ridge.'

'Make sure ya got plenty of shells for them

carbines, boys,' Frank told his men as he pulled out a box of rifle bullets from his saddle-bags and stuffed them into his deep pocket.

Reluctantly, the three new men moved away from their mounts carrying their rifles and ammunition. They walked ahead of Jim and behind Frank. Colt Yancy cradled his Winchester across his waist as Lee Yancy trailed up through the brush after his cousin.

Frank Ritter had deliberately forged a new trail through the trees once they had reached the bottom of the heavily wooded mountainside and headed down into the next valley.

It had been hard to force a tired mount through brush that tore and ripped at its flesh, but Frank knew that he had to create a trail where there had never been one before.

He had to give his gang and himself the upper hand. Frank had known that he had to get away from the narrow trail and into the heart of the forest, where sunlight could hardly penetrate, if he and the rest of his gang were to have any chance of stopping their pursuers.

The seven Winchester-toting outlaws made their way up through the tangled undergrowth towards the spot that Frank Ritter had decided would give them the best chance of bushwhacking the posse behind them.

He, like his cousins, was used to guerrilla warfare after spending so many years with the Quantrill Raiders during and after the war.

There was no terrain that they could not use to their advantage.

If there was one thing that Frank Ritter was an expert at, it was knowing how to get the best out of a bad situation.

And this was a very bad situation.

Blood still dripped from his spurs as he knelt down beside the wide trunk of a tall tree. He looked around as the rest of his men took up the places he had chosen for them.

If the posse did come this way, as the experienced outlaw anticipated they would, they would be torn to ribbons and die in the crossfire.

'This had better work, Frank,' Colt Yancy said, cocking the lever of his repeating rifle.

Frank looked at his cousin and raised his eyebrows.

'Hold that thought, Colt.' He smiled.

'I still reckon that they got themselves a Crow scouting us, Frank,' Lee called out. 'No white man could have followed us this far.'

'Yep. It has to be Walking Horse Man.' Frank spat out the exhausted tobacco plug and wiped his mouth along the back of his jacket sleeve.

'Nobody said nothing about Indians when we joined ya,' Sam Liddle complained angrily.

'Nobody told me that you were a snivelling little brat either, Sam.' Frank riposted. 'Ain't life a real bitch sometimes.'

'You listen to Frank's orders and we'll come through this in one piece, boys,' Jim Yancy chipped in.

'How come?' Tom Parker snapped.

''Coz we was in the war, boy. We was with

92

Quantrill,' Colt shouted. 'Was you in the war?'

'Nope. I was in Nevada.' Parker replied.

'Wish I'd thought about going to Nevada,' Frank said as his wrinkled eyes looked around at the rest of his men. They were spaced roughly ten feet apart behind trees to either side of the crude trail which they had just forged through the dense undergrowth.

'How long before you figure they'll get here?' Jock Johnson asked. His hands were trembling on his Winchester.

Frank bit off a fresh chunk of tobacco and tossed what remained of the bar to the nervous outlaw.

'Take a jawful, Jock. It'll calm ya down.'

Johnson held the tobacco in his shaking hand.

'I ain't scared. You know that I ain't scared, don't you?'

Frank's eyes flashed around his men.

'Make sure them rifles are loaded and ready, boys. That posse ought to be heading over the ridge in less than an hour.'

'An hour?' Colt queried knowingly to his cousin.

'Maybe less,' Frank whispered with a wry smile tracing his hardened features.

His thoughts drifted to his younger brother Jake. He wished that he had him beside him now instead of the trio of new guns.

Jake was worth a dozen such men.

TWELVE

Even on foot, this was a dangerous trail. The line of Pinkerton men carefully led their mounts up the crumbling dusty route after the Crow scout. Dan Larrigan followed the dapple-grey of Walking Horse Man up to the very crest of the mountain ridge. The Indian stopped in his tracks and then crouched down and began dusting the ground with his fingers.

He studied the sun-baked surface with an

intensity that made the rest of the Pinkerton men wonder how he could see anything where they could not.

'Look,' the Crow said pointing at a slight mark in the red dust.

Larrigan knelt, keeping hold of his reins.

'I see a slight mark, Walking Horse Man. Nothing else. What's it mean?'

The Indian rested his hip on the hard ground and stared at the narrow trail which led down through the tall trees until it disappeared a few hundred feet below them.

'The seven riders turned their horses there.' His left hand pointed at the trail below their high vantage point. 'Lead rider not happy to stay on trail and started to move his horse to trees.'

Larrigan squinted into the sun at the forest of trees, which spread out like a green blanket. He could see nothing out of the ordinary.

'You sure?' Larrigan asked.

'You look but Walking Horse Man see, Larrigan.'

There was no sign of any of the outlaws and yet the scout knew exactly where they had gone. Larrigan placed a hand on Walking Horse Man's shoulder.

'You mean to tell me that you figure that they cut off into them trees?'

The Indian nodded.

'They make new trail OK. They try to fool Indian scout.'

Larrigan stood and rubbed his chin.

'I don't like the sound of that.'

The Crow scout kept looking at the ground below them. He seemed to be able to see for miles and yet that appeared to be impossible.

'They try to lead you into place of death,' Walking Horse Man announced.

Larrigan toyed with his reins and pondered the thought. He knew that if anyone could turn the tables on him it was the Ritter and Yancy boys.

'What's wrong, Larrigan?' one of the agents asked as Larrigan, stern-faced, brooded over the information the scout had given him.

'I reckon them Ritter boys are planning to make a stand.'

The men began to sound excited.

'About time. I've been itching to shoot it out with them bastards,' another of the men said, laughing.

Dan Larrigan stared at him.

'Then you're a bigger idiot than you look. The last folks you want to have a showdown with is them boys.'

Suddenly, as the words of the experienced lawman sank in, the ridge fell silent.

THIRTEEN

The seven outlaws heard the approaching horses long before they could make out the fleeting images coming down through the trees. Frank Ritter wondered whether the posse might possibly ride straight into the hastily constructed trap he had set.

It seemed unlikely that Walking Horse Man would lead his followers into a trap, yet the outlaws could hear the horses advancing down the slope towards them.

Had they at last managed to get the better of the posse?

Colt Yancy waved to his brothers and the trio of new men who were secreted behind the broadest trees on the dark slope. Then he looked at his cousin and nodded.

Frank spat at the ground and tucked his Winchester into his shoulder. He stared along its metal shaft through the raised sights.

Soon they would be close enough to pick off, Frank thought.

He glanced at the men around him and nodded.

It was the signal that they had been waiting nearly an hour to see. Each of the outlaws raised his own rifle and trained it on the sound of steadily approaching mounts.

The horses came crashing through the brush above the seven raised Winchesters.

The outlaws squeezed their triggers and fired within seconds of one another. It sounded as if the heavens had exploded.

The bullets tore through the dense undergrowth like crazed fireflies. The sound was deafening and gunsmoke soon filled the entire area.

The sound of horses whinnying filled the outlaw's ears as they kept squeezing their triggers and cranking the mechanisms of their rifles. The heavy bodies of the animals crashed into the trees above them.

Then Frank Ritter's instincts told him that something was not right. He lowered his own rifle, turned his head and shouted at his men. One by one they too stopped firing up the steep mountainside.

With smoke billowing all around them, Colt Yancy was the first to shout back at his cousin.

'What's wrong, Frank? We got 'em licked.'

'I ain't so sure, Colt.' Frank crawled up the steep bushy embankment and leaned his left shoulder against a broad tree. His eyes strained to see their enemy through the gunsmoke, but failed.

'Where are they?' Frank mouthed to the eldest of the Yancy brothers. 'All I see is horses. We've been shooting nothing but damn horses.'

Colt Yancy suddenly felt his blood turn to ice in his veins. He lowered his own Winchester from his shoulder and screwed up his eyes. He stared up at the scene above them and then looked back at Frank Ritter.

'Ya right! The horses are up there but I got me a feeling that their masters ain't.'

'We're in trouble,' Frank growled.

No truer words were ever uttered.

Suddenly, on both sides, the sweating gang heard their enemy. Dan Larrigan had taken heed of the words of Walking Horse Man and realized that they were indeed being lured into a well-set trap. He had made his Pinkerton men dismount just above the new trail forged by the outlaws and split his force into two groups of ten. After sending their mounts down the trail, the detective agents had fanned out to both sides of the trail and made their way through the trees and undergrowth on foot.

Now they had arrived.

Now there were ten well-armed men to either side of the outlaws.

The Pinkerton men were moving in from both sides with their rifles and handguns blazing. Larrigan had been willing to sacrifice some of their mounts to the lethal bullets of the outlaws, for he knew that by the time this bloody encounter was over, his well-armed force would be far fewer in number.

The dark of the forest had defied the bright sun to penetrate its dense canopy for centuries, but now it was being lit up by the blinding flashes of gunfire.

The outlaws felt the heat of the bullets coming at them from both sides. The haunting sounds that the older members of the gang had heard so many times during the merciless war came back to mock them: unforgettable sounds which had been branded into their nightmares for years. The trees all about them were being torn to shreds by the unceasing bullets of their hunters.

It was now they who were being attacked.

'Regroup!' Frank yelled at the top of his voice, trying to make sense of the sudden confusion.

The seven men scrambled to their feet as bullets started to rain in on them with even more intensity from either side of the dense forest.

'What we gonna do?' Sam Liddle cried out. It was the last question he would ever ask. At least half a dozen bullets cut into the young outlaw from both sides. His body seemed to be ripped apart before the eyes of his six companions.

'They got Sam!' Jock Johnson screamed. For the first time since he had first strapped a gunbelt to his hip, he knew what real terror meant.

'Get back to the horses, boys,' Jim Yancy ordered. He cocked and fired his trusty repeating rifle in the direction from where he could see most of the plumes of gunsmoke emanating.

Johnson and Parker did not need telling twice. They ran like scared rabbits whilst the more battle-seasoned Yancys and Frank Ritter divided their fire-power to either side of them as they made a slower, more disciplined retreat.

'What went wrong, Frank?' Colt Yancy asked as he knelt and reloaded his Winchester from the box of bullets in his deep jacket pocket.

'They must have figured out what we were planning,' Frank replied in between rifle shots.

Colt stood and cranked the lever of his rifle. He then raised it and started firing again.

The entire area became filled with the choking acrid stench of smoke as the outlaws continued firing at their still unseen enemy and making their way between the trees back towards the gully and their waiting mounts.

Every few steps they heard the distant screams that told them that at least some of their bullets were finding their unseen targets.

'The bastards let their horses head on down whilst they circled us on foot, Frank,' Lee Yancy shouted as he rested his back against a tree trunk and hastily reloaded his Winchester.

Frank continued firing.

'They're as shifty as we are,' he yelled.

Then it seemed that the entire area was being laced with red-hot tapers as even more rifle bullets sped in from both sides of them. The bark was blasted off the trees all around the four desperate men.

Suddenly Jim groaned and fell on to one knee.

'They got me, boys.'

Frank rushed to his cousin's side and shielded him from further bullets as Colt and Lee hauled their brother back to his feet.

'How is he?' Frank asked through gritted teeth.

'Just winged.' Colt patted his cousin on the back. 'He'll be OK with a bit of doctoring.'

'Get him to the horses, boys,' Frank commanded. 'I'll buy us some time here. Run!'

Lee Younger tossed his loaded weapon into the hands of his cousin.

'Kill a few for me, Frank.'

'I'll sure give it a try, Lee. Now get to the horses.' Frank Ritter cranked the fully loaded rifle, lifted it to hip-height and fired. Then he continued firing where his well-honed instincts told him most of the posse must be.

Again he heard screams.

Then he heard the shouts of men racing through the thick gunsmoke behind him. He turned and blasted three bullets off in quick succession.

The sound of dead men hitting the ground echoed around him.

The posse were getting close, he thought.

Too damn close.

Frank glanced to his side and saw his cousins entering the deep gully. He knew that they would soon be mounted.

Frank Ritter fired one last shot, then

turned and ran down the slope. He had never known himself to be so agile. He darted between the trees as bullets cut chunks of bark off their tall straight trunks.

Hot burning sawdust showered over him but he continued running for all he was worth. He felt the tails of his trail coat being hit by his enemies' bullets but did not hesitate for one second.

He knew that he had to get out of here.

Ritter and his men had killed many of the posse but there were too many more of them out there and they were shooting back at him. Only the thick gunsmoke shielded him as he dived over a hedge and rolled across the slippery ground.

Eventually Frank reached the gully and dragged himself back on to his feet.

The outlaw tossed the rifle into the hands of the mounted Lee and slid his own empty Winchester into its scabbard beneath the saddle horn and threw himself up on top of the black roan. Frantically he gathered in his reins.

He stared around him.

The three Yancy brothers were sitting atop their mounts waiting for him, but Tom Parker and Jock Johnson had already ridden away.

'Where are they? Where's Jock and Tom?'

'They must have been darn scared.' Lee Younger spat at the ground.

'They lit out as if their tails were on fire, Frank,' Colt told his cousin as the four riders made their way along the gully.

With each stride of their mounts' long legs, they could hear the remaining Pinkerton men getting closer. Bullets began to fly over their heads.

'I knew them boys were young but I never took them to be yella rats,' Frank spat out, guiding his horse out of the gully away from the still-deafening rifle fire behind them. 'They done run off and left us to do all the fighting for them.'

'Don't be too hard on them, Frank. They're just young,' Lee said.

'Being young ain't no excuse, Lee,' Frank yelled. 'Jock and Tom will be dead when I catch up with them.'

'Don't waste time fretting over them.' Colt sank his spurs into his mount. 'You gotta figure how we're gonna get out of here.'

Frank looked over his shoulder at the grim faces of his cousins. They were all dependent on his working out how they would make their escape.

'At least that posse will have to catch their horses before they can follow us,' he said. He turned the head of his black roan and forced it through a dense wall of green brush. 'C'mon. We got to make some distance between ourselves and that bunch of backshooters.'

The four horsemen spurred hard and galloped even deeper into the dark forest.

FOURTEEN

The distant sound echoed all around the two horsemen. Cal Hayes pulled back on his reins and looked over his shoulder at the grim-faced Jake Ritter riding behind him. The gunfighter teased his lathered-up horse backward and then hauled it around to face the thoughtful outlaw. There was something in Ritter's eyes that troubled Hayes.

'What's wrong, Jake?'

'Didn't you hear them shots?' Ritter asked. He stood up in his stirrups and stared out across the carpet of treetops below them. It was as if the outlaw was trying to see where the shots had come from.

Hayes leaned forward, rested his gloved hands on top of his saddle horn and tilted his head. He had heard something off in the distance, but was not sure what it was.

'It sounded like thunder to me, Jake.'

Ritter eased himself back down on to his saddle, then lifted his canteen up and unscrewed its stopper. His narrowed eyes flashed at his companion.

'It wasn't thunder, Hayes. It was shooting. A whole heap of shooting.'

Hayes rubbed his chin. The more he thought about it, the more he began to realize that Ritter was right. It had been the sound of shots.

A whole heap of them.

'Where do you figure those shots came from?'

Jake took a mouthful of water, swallowed and then looked at the gunfighter.

'South of here.' The tone of his voice seemed troubled as he slowly replaced the stopper on his canteen and hung it over the saddle horn again. The outlaw gave a huge sigh and then gathered up his reins in his black-gloved hands.

'What's eatin' at ya, Jake? How come you look so bothered?'

Ritter did not answer. He spurred his black roan and then allowed the white-legged animal to walk past Hayes's standing mount.

Reluctantly he replied: 'That's the direction that Frank and the boys should be coming from.'

Hayes could not understand the coldness in his voice. He urged his horse to catch up with the elegant stallion.

'Maybe he's in trouble.'

Ritter glanced at his fellow rider. 'Frank's always in trouble, Hayes. Leastways, when I'm not there to protect him.'

'Ain't you concerned?'

'Nope. Frank can handle himself better than most,' the outlaw answered.

'But the shooting?'

'In our business we get used to folks taking chancy shots at us, Hayes.' Jake continued to walk his mount up the narrowing trail. A wall of rock rose to their right as the horsemen rode slowly up the slope.

'So you ain't even a little worried?'

Jake took a huge sigh. 'I'm always worried

about my kin, but he's got the gang with him.'

'So you figure that he can handle it himself without you getting involved?'

Ritter nodded. They continued up the ridge until they reached the crest of the tree-covered trail. Then Ritter stopped his horse again.

'See it, Hayes?'

Hayes halted his mount, glanced back at their pack-horse, then squinted up to where his friend was aiming his black gloved hand.

'Eagle's Rock!' he exclaimed.

'Damn right.'

No sooner had the words left the outlaw's lips than both men heard a spine-chilling roar above them. Their horses spooked and reared up. The pack-horse bolted.

Cal Hayes was fighting to control his mount when he saw a huge tawny blur pass across his field of vision.

Then he heard Jake Ritter cursing.

When his horse's hoofs grounded on the dusty trail, the gunfighter saw the mountain lion hitting his companion hard.

Jake gave a loud gasp, toppled off his horse and hit the ground. The snarling animal was wrapped around him.

The roar seemed to deafen the gunfighter as Hayes spun his horse around and dragged his Colt Peacemaker from its hand-tooled holster.

He tried to aim but his terrified horse reared up again.

Cal Hayes felt himself falling from his saddle.

Before he landed, he managed to cock the hammer and aim at the snarling puma.

Then Hayes hit the ground.

The gun fired wildly at the very moment that the back of Hayes's skull impacted on the unforgiving trail.

Stunned, the gunfighter watched in horror as the mountain lion leapt off Ritter and started coming towards him.

He tried to move.

It was impossible.

FIFTEEN

Panic was exploding inside the gunfighter's mind. It was unlike anything he had ever experienced before. It was as if the only part of him he could move was his eyes and yet the sight of the ferocious beast twenty feet away from him did nothing but hammer home his own incapacity. Again he tried vainly to move off the hard, dusty ground.

Cal Hayes blinked hard and then realized that the mountain lion was now moving ever closer to him. The roar of the animal seemed to shake the ground beneath his spine, but he was winded and still unable to get up off his back.

He had always thought that pumas were cowardly animals; he had been told that even a loud noise would send them running off. He shouted with every ounce of strength he could muster, to no avail.

Why didn't it work, he wondered.

The eyes of the lion narrowed as it opened its mouth and roared again. Hayes stared hard at the savage teeth and felt his heart pounding even faster.

Then he saw the neat hole in the shoulder of the beast. A spot of dried blood could not conceal that this mountain lion was wounded and angry.

That was why it had attacked!

Hayes's eyes flashed across at the gleaming pistol lying in the sun-baked dust. It lay between his outstretched arm and the vicious beast. He moved his fingers, but he could not reach the weapon.

Then the puma crouched down.

It was ready to pounce on its helpless victim.

Sweat trailed down the side of Hayes's face, but he still could not move a muscle. He felt as if he had been kicked by a mule. All the strength had left his aching body.

'Jake!' he called out desperately.

There was no response.

Hayes could do nothing but lie in the dust and stare into the animal's eyes as it prepared to spring into action. The roaring from the yellow-eyed cat seemed get louder. It was hurt and determined that it would share its own agony with the floored gunfighter.

Suddenly the massive beast leapt like a coiled spring and flew into the air. Its muscular rear legs had pushed it high off the rock-hard ground. It seemed to float across the distance between them like a kite.

Hayes focused his eyes on the large paws of the big cat as they came ever nearer. The claws were at least six inches long and glistened in the sunlight.

The gunfighter wanted to close his eyes.

He had seen enough.

But now he could not even blink.

His wide-open eyes were fixed on the big cat directly over him as it fell towards him.

Then when he was convinced that his short life was all but over, a deafening shot rang out. The cat kept falling towards Hayes.

Then the gunfighter heard another shot just before the mountain lion landed on top of his already bruised body.

It seemed an eternity before Hayes realized that he was not being torn apart by the claws and teeth of the heavy tawny creature which was lying on top of him.

Then a shadow crept across his face.

He stared up at the sight of the bleeding Jake Ritter holding his Schofield in his hand. The barrel was still smoking.

'You saved my bacon, Jake,' Hayes gasped.

'Reckon you owe me one, Hayes.' Ritter raised his right boot and forced the dead animal off his companion. 'If I'd waited another second that lion would have eaten ya.'

'Reckon you're right. He looked a tad hungry.'

'Somebody wounded it with a rifle bullet by the looks of that hole in its shoulder,' Jake said thoughtfully. 'I wonder who?'

'Could be the varmints we've been tracking.' Hayes felt the life coming back into his arms and fingers.

'Big Bill did have a habit of shooting critters just for the fun of it, as I recall,' Ritter said.

Hayes accepted the outstretched black-gloved hand and scrambled to his feet. He dusted himself off and then noticed the deep gashes on the outlaw's chest. The shirt had been ripped from Jake along with much of his skin. Blood was running freely from the fresh wounds.

'You're hurt!' Hayes said. 'You need doctorin'.'

'Damn right. But we got us some kidnappers to catch first, Hayes.' Jake Ritter holstered his gun and then ran his fingers through his hair. As his hair was pushed off his face blood trickled down the side of his temple from a wound high on the side of his head.

'You're head's bleeding as well, Jake,' Hayes said.

Ritter touched the injury and winced.

'That cat sank one of them teeth into my scalp.'

'Does it hurt?' Hayes asked.

Jake sighed.

'Damn right it hurts.'

The gunfighter scooped his hat off the ground and then looked around for their horses. They had galloped a quarter-mile up the trail.

'Looks like we're gonna have to catch our horses, Jake.'

Ritter did not reply. He just stared up at Eagle's Rock.

SIXTEEN

Big Bill O'Mara had jumped to his feet when the sound of the two gunshots echoed around the caves. He moved to the very edge of the cliff and looked down to the trail far below them. He stared hard at the trees, then spotted something that made him growl in anger.

'Get my looking-glasses, Shorty,' he bellowed at the smallest member of his gang.

The outlaw rushed to the saddle-bags and hauled a leather bag out of one of the satchel pouches. He then ran to Big Bill's side and handed him the binoculars case.

Big Bill pulled the expensive binoculars out of the bag and raised them to his eyes. He ran his index finger over the focus wheel.

Then he saw them.

'We got us some company, boys.'

'Who is it?' asked one of the men, named Charter.

'Can't tell. They're too far away for me to make out,' O'Mara replied.

Shorty tugged at Big Bill's raised sleeve.

'Is it the law?'

O'Mara grunted.

'I doubt if the law would ever come up here, Shorty. They ain't dumb.'

'Then who?' asked another outlaw, named Clyde.

'Could be outlaws like us.' Big Bill snorted, staring over his shoulder into the shadows of the cave behind them. 'Maybe they know of the prize we got back there, boys. Might be an ambitious bunch of bandits like us who think they can steal our golden egg out from under our noses.'

Shorty lifted his hand and shielded his eyes from the bright sun.

'Who was they shooting at?'

'It wasn't us.' Charter spat.

'Each other, maybe.' O'Mara shrugged as he tried to get focus his binoculars to get a sharper view of the two figures below them.

'Are they both alive?'

'Yep,' Big Bill answered.

'Then they must have been shooting at someone else.'

'That makes sense, but who?'

Clyde struck a match along his belt buckle, cupped the flame to his cigarette and sucked in the flame.

'You see them horses down there?'

Big Bill grunted.

'Yep. I see them. So what?'

'Is one of them a black roan with four

white stockings going right up to its shoulder, or are my eyes playing tricks on me, Big Bill?' Clyde asked as smoke drifted from his mouth.

O'Mara swung the binoculars round and focused on the three horses on the trail.

'One of them is a black roan, Clyde.'

'There are only two men who ride black roans in this territory, Big Bill.' Clyde looked down at the ground and kicked at the dust with the scuffed toe of his right boot. 'And both of them are called Ritter.'

O'Mara lowered the binoculars from his eyes and looked at the outlaw.

'Frank and Jake?'

Clyde nodded. 'Yep.'

Sweat ran down O'Mara's face as he absorbed the thought of one of the Ritter brothers being so close.

'I heard tell that you and them boys don't get on too well, Big Bill,' Charter said, resting his hands on his guns.

'We've had our differences,' grunted O'Mara.

Clyde blew a line of smoke at the floor.

'Jake once said that he'd kill Big Bill if their paths ever crossed again. Ain't that right, Big Bill?'

O'Mara nodded.

'But you ain't scared of them Ritter boys, are ya?' Shorty asked the man who towered over him.

Big Bill O'Mara did not reply.

He dried his sweating face on the back of his sleeve, handed the binoculars to one of the outlaws and walked into the cooler shadows of the cave.

'What if that is one of the Ritter boys?' Clyde tossed his cigarette away.

The three outlaws watched as O'Mara walked, brooding, up to their saddles and saddle-bags. He was troubled and it showed in his every movement.

Then O'Mara turned.

'Saddle the horses. We gotta get out of here.'

SEVENTEEN

It was a sight that she had not expected. Rose Duggan's face went blank as she watched the four horsemen gallop into the main street of the deserted town. She moved closer to the bedroom window and teased its drape aside to get a better view of the riders.

For one heart-stopping moment she thought that Big Bill O'Mara had returned, then it became clear that the giant outlaw was not one of the horsemen below her bedroom window.

Rose watched as the riders dismounted.

It was obvious to her that one of them was wounded from the way the other three assisted him. She watched as they vainly searched along the street's store fronts for someone to help their riding companion.

Rose knew they were searching for a doctor.

She then studied the four horses tied to a hitching pole almost directly opposite her home. The lathered-up black roan stallion looked familiar. It was almost identical to the one ridden by the man who called himself Jake.

For a fleeting moment she thought that Hayes's friend had returned with three new friends.

Then she realized that the man who rode the magnificent horse was not Jake, although he did resemble Jake slightly. He walked with the same hesitant stride.

Rose was confused and yet unafraid.

Without giving her actions a second thought, she moved out of the bedroom, across the landing and down the stairs towards the open doorway.

She walked out on to the sun-bleached boardwalk and whistled at the four men who were trying every door in order to find a doctor for their bleeding friend.

All four outlaws stopped in their tracks when the sound of her whistle filled their ears.

Swiftly, Frank Ritter turned on his heel and drew his gun with a single swift action. He was taken totally by surprise at the sight of the attractive female.

Their eyes met and the gun was holstered almost as quickly as it had been drawn.

'Hell,' Frank said.

'It's a gal,' Colt Yancy said.

'That's obvious, Colt,' Frank muttered before aiming his steps in her direction.

Rose Duggan stood with her arms folded and did not flinch as the four strangers made their way towards her. Even as they drew closer and closer, she stood firm. If there was any nervousness in her, it didn't show.

'You won't find a doctor in this town, stranger,' she told Frank as he reached the edge of the boardwalk.

Frank smiled.

'Apart from you, we ain't found anyone at all in this town. How come?'

Rose raised one of her perfect eyebrows.

'They all ran away just before Big Bill O'Mara showed up for the third time a few days back.'

Frank stopped a few feet from her and pushed the battered hat off his dust-caked features.

'Big Bill O'Mara.' He repeated the name with a tone in his voice that let her know how he felt about the outlaw.

Rose glanced at the Yancy brothers and then back at Frank.

'Do you know the fat bastard?'

'Yep. Our paths crossed a while back.'

She rested her knuckles on her hips.

'He don't scare me but he sure spooked everyone else in this town.'

'You got nerve, missy,' Colt said loudly.

'Yep.' Rose nodded.

'How come you didn't hightail it with the rest of the folks, ma'am?' Frank was curious.

'I ain't afraid of anyone,' Rose said.

'I reckon not.' Frank glanced over his shoulder at his cousins. He was concerned by the sight of Jim's bleeding, and it showed.

'You need someone to sew him up?' Rose asked, pointing at the weary Jim who was being propped up by his brothers.

Frank removed his hat.

'That would be a kindness, ma'am. If you know of anyone who can tend Jim...'

'I'll sew him up,' she said.

Frank Ritter felt his jaw drop.

'Thanks, ma'am.'

Rose sighed and gestured for Colt and Lee to bring their bleeding brother into her home. She pointed to the back room. It was bathed in sunlight. The Yancys went past her into it.

Frank walked slowly behind the beautiful female and inhaled her natural perfume. It had been a long time since his nostrils had savoured anything so refreshing.

'You done much doctorin' before, ma'am?'

'Nope. But I've done a lot of sewing in my time,' she admitted. She pulled her sewing-kit off a dresser and opened it up. 'I reckon sewing skin together can't be much different from fixing a hide vest.'

Frank did not argue.

Jim was seated at the crude wooden table when she moved closer and inspected the wound beneath the blood-soaked shirt. She pulled out her cutting shears and cut his sleeve off.

'This ain't so bad,' Rose told the trusting outlaw.

Frank rubbed the back of his neck and watched the young female getting down to work.

'Where did you get that fancy horse?' Rose asked as she wiped the blood away from the wound.

None of the men answered until her eyes flashed up and fixed momentarily on Frank Ritter.

'You talking about my black roan?'

'I seen one exactly like it this morning,' Rose said as she cleaned the deep gash with iodine.

Frank moved closer to her.

'You saw another horse like mine?'

'Yep.' Rose threaded her largest needle with catgut.

'Who was riding it, ma'am?'

'A slim stranger who called himself Jake,' Rose replied as she finished threading the darning-needle. 'Come to think of it, he had an accent that was exactly like yours.'

'Jake is my brother.' Frank sighed. 'I was starting to think that something might have happened to him. He was meant to be waiting for us here.'

There was concern in her eyes.

'He was OK the last time I saw him, but things might change if he and Hayes catch up with the gang they're tracking.'

Colt Yancy edged around the table and placed a comforting hand on Jim's shoulder.

'You mentioned Big Bill O'Mara earlier, missy,' Colt said. 'Is he the varmint that Jake and this Hayes character are trailing?'

She nodded.

'But why?' Frank was confused.

'O'Mara and his gang kidnapped the son of an El Paso banker.'

Frank scratched his left eyebrow.

'Jake has had a score to settle with that fat O'Mara for quite some time. Looks like he's out to finish it.'

Colt watched the needle being skilfully woven in and out of his brother's bleeding skin.

'I don't get it. Why would Jake even want to help a banker? He hates bankers more than any other sort of vermin.'

'Who is this Hayes character, ma'am?' Lee asked.

'I'm not sure; he looked like a gunfighter,' Rose muttered as she carefully continued sewing the wound together. 'But Jake seemed to like him.'

Frank sighed heavily, walked to the window and stared out thoughtfully.

'Jake is out to get Big Bill once and for all.'

'But what should we do, Frank?' Lee asked. 'We don't know whether that posse is still on our trail. We ain't got no time to hang around or go looking for Jake.'

Rose looked up at Jim Yancy's face, then

stared around at the other men.

'Are you boys wanted by the law?'

Frank turned and looked at her.

'I'm afraid so.'

'And Jake?' she probed.

'Yep. Jake too,' Frank admitted.

Rose continued to sew up the wounded Jim.

'Ain't that just dandy? This damn town seems to draw outlaws like flies to a dung heap.'

The four men chuckled.

EIGHTEEN

Even though it was late in the afternoon, Cal Hayes could feel the blazing sun burning through the back of his denim jacket as he walked up the steep trail towards their three horses. With every step, he kept thinking about his silent companion behind him.

Jake Ritter had not moved a muscle for more than five minutes since they had encountered the mountain lion. He had just stood like a statue staring up at Eagle's Rock.

Hayes gathered up the reins of the trio of horses, then made his way back down between the tall trees once more.

What was Jake thinking about?

He had never known anyone quite like the legendary outlaw. He knew that in different circumstances he might have been employed to track down him and his gang, to claim the reward money, but as he drew closer to the injured man, that somehow seemed out of the question.

Jake had saved his bacon a dozen or so minutes earlier and that counted for something with the gunfighter. It meant he owed Jake a debt of honour and there was nothing on earth that could wipe that from his thoughts.

He knew that the outlaw could have allowed the puma to kill him, but didn't.

Hayes wondered why. If half the stories

about Jake Ritter were true, he would not have lifted a finger to assist him.

Yet he had. Even with his chest ripped open by the vicious animal's razor-sharp claws, Jake had come to his rescue.

However bad anyone might say Jake was, Hayes knew that he could never again agree. For some unknown reason, the outlaw had taken a shine to him and saved his life.

He still wondered why.

'What you thinking about, Jake?' Hayes asked as he came back to the side of the motionless figure.

Ritter turned his head. His cold eyes, narrowed, stared straight into Hayes's face.

'You say something, Hayes?'

'I asked what you was thinking about.' Hayes repeated the question.

'I was thinking about Big Bill and his cohorts.' Ritter pulled out his silver cigar-case, removed the last of his large Havanas and bit off its tip. 'They know that we're here.'

'How do you know that?'

'Someone up there in the mouth of one of the caves has been watching us with binoculars,' Ritter replied. 'I've been watching the sun flashing off the lenses.'

Hayes held on to the reins and glanced up at the distinctive rock formation.

'I thought you was just thinking. I never seen anyone think for quite so long.'

Ritter nodded.

'I did me some thinking as well.'

'What about?'

'I like to get things straight in my head before I act, Hayes.' Jake placed the long brown cigar between his teeth and returned the empty case to his inside breast pocket. 'Me and O'Mara go back a long time.'

'You got a beef with O'Mara?'

Ritter struck a match and lit the cigar. He puffed for a few seconds and kept staring up at Eagle's Rock.

'We have a score to settle. I've been chasing that fat swine for an awful long time and now I can smell him. Yep. We got us a score to settle.'

135

'I thought that you came with me to help me get the banker's son away from them cutthroats?' Hayes wondered whether the outlaw had ridden with him for reasons other than the one that he had first claimed.

Was this simply a chance for Ritter to get revenge on the evil Big Bill O'Mara?

'I'll help you get that boy away from them, Hayes,' Jake said as he turned and accepted the reins to his black roan. 'But you have to understand that me and Big Bill go back an awful long way. We have a lot of grief to wage on one another. The Bible says "an eye for an eye". He owes me an eye.'

'I don't get it,' Hayes admitted.

'Big Bill was one of the bastards who was with the varmints who threw a bomb into my mother's house, Hayes,' Ritter recalled woefully. 'She lost an arm and I lost me a kid brother.'

'I read about that a long time ago.'

'So did I. The Pinkerton men bombed her house and me and Frank were a hundred miles away, Hayes.' Jake flicked the ash off his cigar and licked his lips. 'But they had the law on their side, so it was legal.'

'Sometimes the law is an ass.'

Ritter stared through the cigar smoke. 'I've managed to get a few of the swine who killed little Archie and crippled my mother, but Big Bill has always managed to keep well out of my way. They reckon that he told the Pinkerton men that we were there just to get my kin killed.'

Cal Hayes knew that there was a fury burning inside the outlaw that he could not even imagine.

'So you're out to make him pay?'

'Damn right.' Jake Ritter stepped into his stirrup and hauled himself up on to his saddle. He pointed up at Eagle's Rock.

'We ought to get there well before sundown, Hayes.'

'Damn right.' Hayes grinned as he mounted. Ritter tapped his spurs into the side of his black roan stallion and started through the trees on the final stage of their journey.

'That happens to be a good hideout, but it does have one major drawback,' Ritter said as Hayes drew level with him, holding the reins of their pack-horse at his side.

'What's that?'

Ritter sucked on his cigar. 'There's only one safe route in and out of them crags.'

'Maybe they've already headed out,' Hayes suggested. 'You did say that someone was watching us.'

Jake glanced at his companion.

'It takes an awful lotta time to saddle up and head down from up there.'

'How much time, Jake?'

'Enough time for us to intercept them on the trail.'

Both riders continued heading through the tall straight trees towards their destiny.

NINETEEN

Jake had been right as usual. The sun had not quite slipped beneath the horizon when they rode out from the dense forest on to the stony trail, but it was nearly gone.

Hayes reined in and stared at his fellow horseman. Again, the outlaw seemed to be totally absorbed in something that the gunfighter could neither see nor hear.

Ritter was holding his stallion in check and listening to every sound that drifted around the eerie trail. It was obvious that he had been here many times before.

'What is it, Jake?' Cal Hayes asked. He pulled his mount up short beside the thoughtful Ritter, who was standing in his stirrups.

'Hush up,' Ritter ordered.

Then, without saying a word, Ritter

dismounted and led his black roan back into the cover of the brushwood.

Hayes turned his horse and followed. He knew that this was a man who had remained one step ahead of the law and alive because he had honed his instincts to be aware of everything around him.

It was getting darker with every passing heartbeat. Hayes slid off the back of his mount and led it and the pack-horse to where the outlaw was securing his black roan.

'What's wrong, Jake?'

The outlaw shook his head in disbelief.

'Are you deaf? Can't ya hear them coming, Hayes?'

'I must be deaf, I can't hear a thing.' Cal Hayes knotted the heavy leather reins to a stout tree-branch and then ran beside the outlaw back to the edge of the steep rocky trail road.

'Listen,' Ritter whispered.

The gunfighter knelt at the edge of the bushes beside Ritter and strained his ears to hear. At first he could hear nothing except the countless birds who were mourning the passing of another day. Then he finally managed to make out the sound of horses' hoofs rattling on the rough trail above them.

'I hear them.'

'At last.' Ritter sighed.

Darkness seemed to be enveloping them far faster than either man had imagined it would. Hayes wondered if it was the sheer height of the trees surrounding their hiding-place that made it impossible for the sunlight to reach them. Whatever the reason for its apparently getting dark so fast, it didn't alter the fact that it was.

'Damn!' Jake Ritter snarled as he pulled his Smith & Wesson out of its holster and cocked its hammer. 'I hate having a shoot-out at night.'

Hayes pulled his Peacemaker from its resting place in the hand-tooled holster and pulled back on its hammer. It clicked three times before fully locking into position.

'If there was a moon we might be able to

see the bastards coming,' Hayes whispered.

'I know.' Ritter sighed, resting the gun on his knee as he knelt beside a broad tree-trunk and stared around it. The shadows seemed to be engulfing the entire mountain range as they waited.

'I don't want to open up on them riders and risk hitting the kid that you've gotta rescue.'

'What'll we do?'

Jake Ritter rested his chin on his knuckles and tried to think of a way that they could be sure to get the right men and not kill an innocent victim. Blackness was surrounding them like a cloak. It covered everything.

He kept thinking about his half-brother dying all those years back in his mother's home. He had done many things in his time but he had never risked the lives of innocent people knowingly and had no intention of starting now.

The sound of the horses grew louder as the echoes of their hoofs bounced off all the encircling trees. The ground beneath them began to tremble.

'We can't risk it, Hayes,' Ritter said. He released the hammer of his gun and slid it back into its holster.

Hayes looked at his companion blankly.

'What?'

'There ain't no way we can stop them here,' Ritter amplified. 'If the sun was still with us, it would be different. But it ain't.'

'Then where do you suggest we can stop them?'

Ritter placed his hand on Hayes's gun arm. Within seconds the outlaws and their hostage thundered past them. Dust kicked up all over the two kneeling men. But neither had been able to make out any of the riders.

Jake knew that Big Bill O'Mara was cunning enough to vary his position when riding with his gang. Sometimes he led them and on other occasions he would ride second or even last. Jake also knew that it was not beyond the realms of possibility for O'Mara to make their hostage lead the way, so if anyone did try to stop them, it would be he who got shot first.

They rose to their feet and listened to the riders making their way down the mountain.

'We have to trail them, Hayes.'

'In the dark?'

'It ought to be easy 'coz there's only one place that they can head to from here.' Ritter walked back to their horses.

'You figure they're headed back to the deserted town?' Cal Hayes asked.

'I'll bet you a new hat that it ain't deserted now.' Ritter began to remove his saddle from his horse.

'I know Rose is there.'

The outlaw dropped the saddle on to the ground and then sat down on it.

'If Frank and the boys are still alive they should have gotten there by now.' Jake sighed. 'Big Bill is like the meat in a sandwich, only he's too dumb to know it.'

'How come you've unsaddled ya mount?' Hayes asked, pushing his Colt into its holster. 'We've gotta catch up with them push kidnappers.'

'We're making camp and having us some hot vittles first. Then we'll head on out after them. They'll be hungry and we'll be rested up.'

Cal Hayes shrugged and lifted up his fender and hooked the stirrup on to the saddle horn. He started to unfasten his cinch straps.

'Are you cooking or am I?'

'You are,' Ritter replied. 'I'm Jake Ritter, I'm used to taking risks.'

TWENTY

The light of six blazing torches illuminated the small clearing on the forested slope. The haunting dancing shadows had done nothing to lessen the impact of the scene of carnage that had stopped the Pinkerton men in their tracks. Even now, two hours after the brief but brutal battle, the odour of death still lingered.

Dan Larrigan was a man whose entire life in the service of the law followed a single code. A code of honour. It had cost him dearly over his long blood-soaked career, and yet he still remained true to what he believed was right.

Men like Larrigan could not be easily swayed from what they saw as their chosen destiny. He only existed to administer the law.

He also knew that this bloody encounter had taken its toll on his meagre force of so-called agents. A far bigger price had been paid than he had ever imagined.

The Ritter–Yancy gang had somehow managed to thwart his well-planned attack. Whether it had been sheer luck or real skill mattered little in the end. It had been his Pinkerton agents who had been cut down and not the notorious outlaws.

Dan Larrigan knew he had to continue following the trail of the ruthless gang and make them pay.

Now, even more than before, they had to be brought to justice.

He had lost eight of his original force and another five were badly wounded. He had already dismissed the notion of taking his dead home. He knew the journey was too long.

The dead had been buried where they had fallen. To Larrigan, it was the only way.

Apart from himself and Walking Horse Man, he had only five able-bodied Pinkerton agents left and none of them wanted to continue their dangerous quest in following the Ritter–Yancy gang any further into this unknown terrain.

Larrigan folded up the small shovel, slid it into his saddle-bags and then rested his head on the cold leather of the saddle seat. He was physically exhausted but not ready to quit whilst there was still breath in his body.

He had spent hours digging the graves alone. None of the men who were still alive wanted to help.

They only wanted to get back on their

horses and return to their various offices and homes. Places that lay far away from this forest and the stench of gunsmoke and death.

Larrigan forced himself away from his mount and then turned to face the unruly band who had the nerve to call themselves Pinkerton men.

As he had dreaded, they had let him down and most had paid the ultimate price.

'I have orders to track this gang down and either capture them or kill them,' Larrigan said bluntly. 'I think that the latter option is the more favourable.'

Not one of the seated men before him opened his mouth. He had led them into a trap and that was something they could not forget or forgive. None of them was willing to even consider taking this one step further.

They would kill him rather than stay on the trail of the infamous gang of outlaws, and Dan Larrigan knew it.

Larrigan pointed at the graves.

'Are we going to allow those bastards to get away with this slaughter, boys?'

Again, there was nothing but silence.

Larrigan moved closer to the grim faces that stared at him with hate in their eyes.

'I want you men to follow me. I know where they're headed.'

Agent Slim Cooper got up off the ground and looked straight into the eyes of the exhausted Larrigan.

'You're tuckered out, Dan. We're all tuckered out,' Cooper said in a cold dispassionate voice as he waved his hand at the shallow graves. 'I figure that if we keep trailing them, they'll finish us all off just like they done with these boys.'

'But we're Pinkerton men,' Larrigan shouted.

'So were they.' Cooper pointed at the graves again. 'We don't wanna end up like them. These tin stars don't stop any bullets and they don't guarantee that we'll win.'

'Are you all yella?' Larrigan shouted at the top of his voice. He clenched his blistered fists. 'Are you scared of Jake Ritter and Colt Yancy?'

'We ain't yella, Dan,' Cooper said. 'We just ain't ready to get ourselves killed for what Allan Pinkerton pays.'

The rest of the men rose to their feet and helped their wounded comrades up off the hard bloodstained ground. Silently they headed back towards what was left of their horses. None of them looked back at the dejected Dan Larrigan.

The tall man watched the men disappear into the darkness, beyond where the light of the torches could reach. He turned and looked at the silent figure of Walking Horse Man.

The Crow scout moved to the side of the confused Larrigan and rested a hand on his shoulder.

'I told you that there would be no winners in this battle, Larrigan. This is a fight that cannot be won, for the men you seek are too good at killing. They have big magic protecting them.'

'Reckon you must be right, Walking Horse Man,' Larrigan admitted. 'But it just don't sit well with me. I like to finish a job once I've started it. I ain't no quitter.'

'It is the madness of the white-eyes to keep fighting when the war is lost.' Walking Horse Man sighed. 'Pride has killed more warriors than arrows have.'

'Guess I must be plumb loco then, 'coz I'm gonna keep following that gang until I get them or they get me.' Larrigan sighed heavily.

The Indian nodded.

'It is a madness I understand.'

'You do?'

Walking Horse Man nodded.

'Once the warriors of my tribe were like the leaves on the trees in summer, but then the Sioux came and made war. Then the white-eyes came and nothing was ever the same again. Now my people are like the buffalo.'

'I ain't seen a buffalo in ten years, Walking Horse Man.'

'They are gone, like my people.'

Dan Larrigan knew that they were both a dying breed. Their time had long since passed into history.

'You've been a good friend to me over the years. Reckon we might not see one another again.'

The scout raised a hand to his chest and placed it over his heart.

'I will go with you to show you the trail, Larrigan. We shall face our fate together.'

Larrigan patted Walking Horse Man on the back.

'Thanks, old friend.'

TWENTY-ONE

Neither rider had noticed the sun rising as they continued to steer their mounts down the hard rocky trail after Big Bill O'Mara and his henchmen. Jake Ritter had led the way from Eagle's Rock atop his sturdy black roan with a determination that Cal Hayes found hard to match or understand.

Neither man had managed to sleep during the time that they had allowed their horses to rest below the caves of Eagle's Rock. But they had eaten their first hot meal for days before resuming their journey.

As the rocky ground beneath their horses' hoofs levelled out and they were faced with one last tree-covered mountain, the outlaw slowed his horse to a halt.

Hayes drew alongside and reined in. Looking over his shoulder he checked the pack-horse. He had tied its reins to his saddle fender.

Jake gazed at the twisting trail that cut up the massive green barrier before them and frowned. It looked bigger with the sun casting its light across it.

'I let them back-shooters get too far ahead of us, Hayes,' he reluctantly admitted. 'I don't think that we can catch up with them before they reach the town.'

'If that's where they're headed, Jake.'

'Seems a reasonable bet.'

The gunfighter lifted his canteen off his

saddle horn and slowly unscrewed its stopper. He too stared up at the thicket of trees and felt the hairs beneath his bandanna making him itch. It was obvious that the men they sought had long since managed to clear the crest of the mountain and were on their way down the other side by now.

'Then what'll we do if we can't catch up with them?'

Jake Ritter removed his Stetson and rubbed the sweat from his brow across his sleeve. His eyes were searching the landscape before them, looking for something that would give him an answer. He shielded his eyes from the morning sun with his wide hat-brim and squinted to their right.

'I could be wrong, but that looks like a valley over there,' Ritter said. 'What do you reckon?'

Hayes stood in his stirrups and gazed at the distant dip beyond the trees.

'You could be right.'

'Look at them birds roosting on the trees over there, Hayes,' Ritter said. 'In my book, that means that there's a creek or river down there. Where there's running water, there just has to be a route around this mountain. Water always runs downhill, don't it?'

'Seems to make sense. I ain't never heard of water flowing up a hill,' Hayes agreed.

'You figure it's worth a bet for us to take a look?'

Cal Hayes nodded. 'And if there's a river, we can use it to cut around this mountain, Jake.'

Ritter replaced his hat on his head and pulled the brim down to shield his eyes from the morning sun.

'Even if it's a dry valley, we could still cut through there and save ourselves a couple of hours getting to the town. We might even catch up with O'Mara before he gets there.'

Hayes took a long swallow from his canteen, then handed it to his companion.

'It would save us having to ride back over that damn mountain again, if nothing else, Jake.'

'What if I'm wrong and it don't lead out to

the range?' Ritter asked. He took a sip from the canteen then returned it to the gunfighter. 'We would have to retrace our tracks and lose hours. What if I am wrong?'

'Jake Ritter wrong?' Hayes screwed the stopper back on his canteen and hung it over the saddle horn. 'Ain't that impossible?'

'Damn right.' The outlaw grinned, hauled his reins hard to his right and spurred his mount. Hayes drove his horse on after the dust of the black roan's hoofs. The two horsemen cut across the almost level ground towards the place which they both prayed would be a valley that they could use to save them some time.

The horses soon found a pace that neither had been able to exercise since entering this land of high twisting trails. Both riders encouraged their faithful mounts on across the flat ground towards the place where hundreds of birds were roosting.

The thundering hoofs ate up the ground before the two riders eased back on their reins and stared down at the crystal-clear water flowing beneath the dense canopy of tree branches before them.

'Feel lucky, Hayes?'

'Now I do.'

Ritter spurred his black roan and entered the shallow creek first. Hayes was more cautious as he led their pack-horse into the ice-cold water.

Both horsemen followed the course of the creek at a speed that neither man would have even contemplated in any other circumstances.

But they were in a hurry.

They had to try to catch up with O'Mara and his gang before they disappeared out on the vast tree-covered range.

There was no time to lose.

TWENTY-TWO

The tension was rising as quickly as the sun above the heads of the five riders who were making their way down the mountain trail towards the tree-covered range. Big Bill O'Mara had led his men, and the securely tied Joseph McCabe, half-way down the forested trail when something alerted him to danger ahead.

With the razor-sharp instincts that had kept him alive far longer than anyone of his sort deserved, he dragged back on his reins and stopped his mount in its tracks. The other riders behind him bumped into the rear of his stationary horse as the hefty outlaw hauled his Winchester from its leather scabbard beneath his saddle.

O'Mara knew that at least one of the Ritter brothers had been trailing him and his gang from Eagle's Rock, but this new danger was ahead of him.

'What is it, Bill?' Charter asked.

O'Mara did not say a word as he pointed the long barrel of his rifle at faint plumes of smoke twisting their way up through the tops of the trees. He dismounted and gave his reins to Shorty before cranking the mechanism of the repeating rifle as quietly as he could.

His nostrils had detected the aroma of burning kindling long before his eyes had caught a brief glimpse of the wisps of smoke that managed to crawl out from the trees.

'Whoever that is, they're gonna die,' Big Bill muttered to his men.

Charter slid from his saddle and stood beside the head of the horse upon which they had tied their hostage. He glanced up at the young man's face. It was still heavily bruised from the beatings they had inflicted upon him. Only the eyes of Joseph McCabe remained uncovered from bindings.

'Keep looking, rich boy.' Charter grinned.

'You might just see how deadly Big Bill is with that carbine.'

Joseph struggled vainly against his restraints. Even he could not work out why these men had not killed him yet. But he was still more valuable alive than dead to his captors, who knew that they could milk his father dry before eventually killing him. If he was alive, they could always send fresh parts of his body to the El Paso banker to encourage the elderly gentleman to part with more and more money.

To kill him in this heat would be to invite a hundred vultures to dog their trail.

'What's going on, Charter?' Clyde asked his fellow-outlaw as he leaned down from his saddle.

'Big Bill has seen something,' Charter replied quietly, holding on to the bridle of the horse.

Clyde smiled and then straightened up.

'Then I reckon that somebody is gonna die darn soon.'

Charter nodded in silent agreement.

Defying his enormous bulk, Big Bill moved his hefty frame through the brush like a puma. He had sensed that there was someone ahead of them and, as he closed in on his target, his eyes confirmed his suspicions.

Jock Johnson and Tom Parker had known that they were lost even before they had reached this place. But at least they were no longer being shot at by the posse who had followed them relentlessly day after day.

Two men were crouched over a crude campfire, trying to keep its pathetic flames going. These were not seasoned men, used to the great outdoors like O'Mara. They did not even have the brains to know that you did not put damp kindling on a fire unless you wanted to make smoke rather than flames. But they were also hungry and desperate to get something hot into their bellies.

'Frank will kill us for sure if'n he catches up with us, Jock,' Tom said as he emptied the contents of his saddle-bag on to the ground next to the fire, searching for something that could be cooked.

'I don't give a damn,' Johnson snarled. 'We hired on to rob a bank, not get ourselves executed.'

Above them, O'Mara leaned against a tree-trunk and steadied the rifle in his grip. He then searched the surrounding area for signs of more men.

There was none.

Whoever these men were, they were alone.

Big Bill could see their two lathered-up horses tied up below him.

Neither horse would have made a decent pot of glue between them, he thought. They had been run to exhaustion and it showed.

Big Bill returned his attention to the two men. They were as green as the twigs that they kept placing on top of the pathetic camp-fire. Smoke arched its way out of the small clearing and tracked its way heavenward.

O'Mara thought to himself: soon the two men's souls would also be heading in that direction.

Big Bill O'Mara focused his gaze through

the raised sights of the Winchester. He trained the rifle barrel on the back of Jock Johnson.

He then fired and recranked the rifle lever.

The rifle shot was deafening as the bullet tore into Johnson's coat. Blood burst like an erupting volcano from the man's chest as the lethal lead pierced through his body.

Johnson fell across the camp-fire, sending smoke billowing over his stunned companion.

Tom Parker rolled away from the fire and drew his Colt .45 from its holster. He fired back into the thicket of trees. He then heard another shot. He felt his left shoulder shattering before he was thrown into a bush by the impact.

Parker lay on his back and clawed at the hammer of his gun with his thumb. It finally locked.

Another rifle bullet then hit him in his side.

Tom Parker could taste the blood filling his mouth. He managed to stagger back to his feet, then he spotted the burly figure coming at him through the brushwood.

Parker raised his gun and tried to aim.

Then he saw the gunsmoke spewing from the barrel of the Winchester rifle.

When the bullet hit him dead centre, he was lifted off his feet. He crashed into a tree and watched as the rifleman fired again. Blood poured from Parker's open mouth and drenched what was left of his body. He stared down at his pistol and then fell on to his face.

O'Mara laughed at the sight of his bloody handiwork.

'Who were they, Bill?' Charter called out as he watched the burly man kicking the lifeless bodies over.

Big Bill had no idea who they were, but it mattered little to the outlaw, who was stripping them of their weapons and personal possessions.

He was like a vulture tearing the last fragments of his victims' identities to shreds.

Frank Ritter and Colt Yancy came out of the

house and stood beneath the porch over-hang. Frank stood on the boardwalk outside Rose's home and grabbed Colt Yancy's arm. His blood ran cold as the echoes of distant shots continued to resound around the otherwise silent town.

'Hear that? Did you hear that, Colt?'

'Yep. I heard. Reckon that there are a few folks out there having themselves a show-down.'

Frank glanced at his cousin.

'Showdown or ambush? Jake's out there someplace.'

Colt nodded. 'I'll get our horses and you and me can go take us a ride out there and have a look.'

Frank Ritter lowered his head and sighed. He knew that his brother was out there amid the forest of tall trees with the stranger called Hayes. He also knew that Big Bill O'Mara was out there with his gang and the hostage he had snatched from El Paso.

'Nope. We stay here, Colt. We stay here and we wait.'

Colt moved around until he was standing directly in front of his troubled cousin. He tried to look into the eyes that he had known all his life and yet the man refused to do anything but look at the ground.

'But Jake might be in trouble, Frank,' Colt began. 'What if this Hayes character turned on him for the reward money? We don't know what's happening out there.'

'We do,' Frank corrected. 'Somebody was shooting.'

'But who and why?' There was genuine concern in the outlaw's face.

'Whoever was shooting is probably headin' this way anyway. All we gotta do is wait.' Frank Ritter stepped down into the street and walked, with his cousin at his side, to a narrow alley opposite Rose Duggan's home.

Colt rubbed his unshaven jaw.

'How can you be so certain that anyone will head here, Frank?'

Frank Ritter raised his right arm and pointed with his trigger finger out at the range.

'Look.'

Colt Yancy narrowed his eyes and stared hard out at the distant dust that was rising into the blue sky. Even the shimmering heat haze could not disguise the fact that riders were heading towards them at incredible speed.

'Who is that?'

Frank tilted his head and looked at Colt.

'We better pray that it's Jake and Hayes. If it's Big Bill O'Mara and his boys, we're in trouble.'

'We can handle O'Mara.'

'On a good day you'd be right.' Frank raised his hand again and pointed south at the trail that they had taken to reach this place hours earlier. Dust was also rising into the sky in that direction as well. 'But with the posse headin' in as well, this ain't a good day.'

'What'll we do, Frank?'

Frank spat at the ground.

'We're gonna wait, Colt.'

TWENTY-THREE

The sky looked as if it were aflame as the sun hung low above the small town. Frank Ritter and his cousins had taken refuge in the front rooms above the deserted saloon a few buildings down the street from the house in which the stubborn Rose Duggan had remained.

They had waited for hours in the hot rooms, staring out of its open windows over the second-floor balcony which stretched the entire length of the wooden building.

Then they saw the dust of horses being reined in drift along the deserted street below their vantage point. It was a lot of dust. That meant it had to be more than two riders who had just ridden into the street.

Frank had known that if it was Big Bill and his cronies who showed up first, they would head for the saloon to quench their thirst.

'Who do you figure it is, Frank?' the wounded Jim Yancy asked from the easy-chair in which he had been resting since they had taken up temporary residence in the saloon's private quarters.

Frank leaned against the window frame and tried to see up the street, but it was impossible.

'I'd have to poke my head out of one of these windows to know the answer to that, Jim,' Frank replied. 'And I don't intend giving anyone an excuse to part my hair with a bullet just yet.'

Colt and Lee had gathered every piece of their arsenal together just in case they needed it. Boxes of ammunition for their various weapons were scattered all around the two rooms which fronted the saloon's upper level.

'Ya hear anything, Frank?' Lee asked as he sat on the floor loading every rifle and gun before him.

Frank nodded. 'Voices.'

'Does it sound like Jake?' Jim accepted an

extra gun from his brother and tucked it into his belt.

'Nope.' The answer came quickly as Frank teased the lace drape away from the window and looked through the gap.

Colt moved to the side of his brooding cousin.

'We should have hightailed it out of here.'

Frank ignored the remark and then tapped Colt's arm with his hand.

'Whoever they are, they're headed this way,' he informed his cousins. 'Best try not to make any noise once they bust their way inside.'

'I ain't scared of Big Bill,' Jim said.

'Neither am I. I just want them to have a few snorts downstairs before we introduce ourselves.' There was a wry smile on Frank's face as he allowed the lace drape to fall back. He stood looking down, knowing that he could see and not be seen.

'I reckon we ought to go down there with guns blazing, Frank,' Lee said. He got to his feet with his hands full of extra sixguns. 'Big

Bill deserves to be killed.'

Frank raised a finger to his lips. It was a silent order to be quiet which his three cousins obeyed without question.

The five horses soon came into view.

Big Bill O'Mara was riding at the back of the quintet of sweating mounts. He still looked stalwart and as cunning as he had always done.

Frank studied the group carefully. He recognized Charter from a few years earlier, when the outlaw had vainly tried to join his and Jake's gang.

Clyde and Shorty were unknown to him.

Then he spotted the pathetic, gagged figure of Joseph McCabe, who was trussed up on his saddle with little enough rope to ensure that he could not move a single muscle.

Frank rubbed his lips and then pointed at the banker's son.

'Looks like the dude that Jake was after with Hayes,' he whispered to Colt.

'That don't look so good to me, Frank,' Colt said. He looked worried. 'If Jake and

Hayes were out to rescue that youngster, and he's still hogtied atop that horse, maybe we got us an answer to who it was got themselves shot earlier.'

Frank Ritter went pale.

'Can't be. Jake could outshoot any of them. You don't think that they could have gotten the better of Jake, do ya?'

Cole bit his lip.

It seemed impossible even to consider it but he had always been a realist. Could O'Mara have managed to get the drop on Jake Ritter?

'You don't really think that, do ya, Colt?' Frank was staring straight into his cousin's face.

'I sure hope not, Frank,' Colt said. 'If they did, they would have had to bushwhack him.'

'If I find out that they bushwhacked Jake, I'll cut out their lily-livered hearts.' Frank returned his eyes to the dismounting men below them in the street. The sky was now even redder and casting its devilish light across the town. But it was not the reflected crimson light that tinted his eyes.

There was a fire raging inside Frank Ritter. Every heartbeat only added to its ferocity.

The men listened as they heard the sound of the boards being torn from the front door of the saloon. Then they heard the ear-splitting sound of a well-placed bullet shattering its padlocked doors.

'They're inside, Frank,' Colt said quietly.

The sound of whiskey bottles being pulled off shelves in the heart of the saloon below them filled their ears.

'They're drinking, just like you said they would, Frank.' Lee grinned at his cousin.

Frank listened, nodded knowingly to himself for a few moments. Then he looked at his cousins' faces. One by one he stared into their eyes and winked.

'Remember, I get to kill Big Bill.'

The three Yancy brothers followed their cousin towards the door that led to the landing high above the stale-smelling saloon. Then they heard the sound of gunfire coming from out in the street.

They turned, rushed back to the windows and looked out into the street. The unmistakable black roan stallion and its equally recognizable master were in the centre of the street, a hundred yards from the saloon.

Another shot echoed around the wooden buildings. The four heads turned to look at Cal Hayes, sitting on his mount a hundred yards away in the opposite direction.

Frank squinted at both men. Then he went out on to the balcony. His cousins soon followed him through the open windows.

'Jake and that *hombre* are trying to draw the bastards out of the saloon.' Frank grinned.

'What'll we do?' Colt asked.

Frank swung around on his heels. 'That kid that Big Bill has tied up down in the bar must be mighty important to Jake if he's willing to get into a showdown with them.'

'C'mon, boys. O'Mara won't expect anyone to get the drop on him from up here. We might be able to snatch the kid out from under their noses.' Colt nudged the gang.

They all scrambled back into the windows and made their way quietly on to the landing.

Frank Ritter pulled out his handguns, cocked their hammers and waited on the balcony. If any one of Big Bill's gang poked their heads out below him, he was ready to put a bullet into every one of them.

Colt Yancy edged his way along the far wall of the landing with his brothers close behind him. He pointed at the floor and Jim knelt down with his guns cocked and readied.

Then Colt and Lee made their way to the top of the wide staircase. It was dark inside the saloon with all its window shutters nailed tight. At first they could not see where the men they sought were.

It was Lee who spotted the seated figure of Joseph McCabe directly below them. He was still tied up like a spring calf waiting to be branded.

Colt nodded when Lee pointed the barrel of one of his weapons at the helpless figure.

Then, as their eyes adjusted to the lack of light, they saw the four outlaws near the open front doors.

Two more shots from out in the street made Big Bill and his gang jump. Vainly they tried to see who was trying to draw them out of the safety of their refuge.

'Who in tarnation is out there, Bill?' Clyde asked, his hands holding on to his cocked Remingtons.

The hefty outlaw looked at the least favourite of his men and snarled.

'Why don't ya go take a look, Clyde?'

The outlaw felt the beefy hands grabbing the back of his vest as he was thrown out of the doorway into the street. He rolled out on to the sand and then saw the two horsemen at either end of the street.

He raised both his guns and fired. Then a thunderous volley came from above. Clyde staggered backwards for almost ten feet before his legs buckled and he fell lifeless on to the sand.

Big Bill spat angrily.

'There's someone up on the balcony,' he growled.

Colt and Lee Yancy had walked down the carpeted stairs without being seen or heard. They were about to call out to O'Mara when the big man turned and spotted them.

'Duck!' Lee shouted to his brother as the outlaws near the door opened up with their lethal lead.

The two brothers dived sideways into the stale sawdust. Colt managed to get behind the end of the long bar just as bullets tore into the hand-carved mahogany. Lee crawled behind the cast-iron heating-stove just as half a dozen bullets bounced off its black surface.

The brothers returned the fire.

'We gotta get out of here!' O'Mara shouted as hot lead sped in their direction. Splinters showered over the trio of gunmen as they charged out on to the boardwalk into the street.

'That was the Yancy brothers, Bill,' Charter shouted above the sound of the gunfire that was still coming out of the open doorway beside them.

Big Bill's eyes narrowed.

'That means the Ritter boys must be around here,' he growled at Shorty and Charter. 'Them bastards are kin. They don't go no place without each other.'

'You got a beef against the Ritter boys, Bill?' Charter asked innocently.

The large man spat and fired two shots into the saloon. He had to keep the Yancys at bay long enough for him to think.

'Yeah, I got me a beef against them Ritter brothers,' O'Mara answered angrily. 'Them bastards used to be a thorn in my side a long time ago back in Missouri. Every damn bank I tried to raid, them boys robbed first. They had the luck of the Irish and made me look a fool. Nobody makes Big Bill look foolish. So when I heard tell that they was staying with their mother on her farm in Morganstown, I got in touch with the Pinkerton boys. They kinda turned a blind eye to all my lawbreakin' as long as I led them to the farm.'

'You squealed on them?' Shorty's eyebrows rose in disbelief.

'Right enough, Shorty. I led them Pinker-

178

ton greenhorns right up to the front door of that farmhouse.'

'What happened?'

'Them detectives just pussy-footed around for the longest time calling out for Jake and Frank to come on out, but their mother just kept screaming that they weren't there. So I kinda put the fox in the henhouse.'

'How'd ya mean?'

Big Bill O'Mara grinned. 'I had me some munitions left over from the war and one of them accidentally went through the window and blew the place apart. The old lady had her arm blown off and her son got himself killed.'

'No wonder the Ritter boys don't like you, Bill.' Shorty sniffed.

'They ain't never proved nothing against me, Shorty.' O'Mara spat again.

Suddenly, Shorty grabbed at O'Mara's sleeve and pointed up the street at the black roan stallion standing without its master in its saddle.

Big Bill rubbed the sweat off his face with

his sleeve and stared at the horse. He knew that both Jake and Frank rode such rare animals.

He gulped. 'That black roan must be Jake's horse, but where is the snivelling coward?'

Then Charter pointed at the other end of the street. Now Cal Hayes's horse was also standing without its master astride it as the eerie rays of the fading red light spread across the wooden buildings.

More bullets traced through the air from inside the saloon, shattering the glass in the boarded-up windows beside the three outlaws.

'Where the hell are they? Where'd they go?' O'Mara's voice was unusually desperate. He could feel the heat of his enemies' bullets getting closer and closer.

Charter shook his head.

'I ain't staying here to get myself killed. I'm outa here.'

O'Mara watched the outlaw holster his guns and leap off the boardwalk on to the saddle of his horse. Before he had time to haul his reins off the hitching pole another bullet came from the balcony above him. Charter's head exploded, sending him cartwheeling off his saddle on to the ground.

'Charter's dead, Big Bill!' Shorty screamed.

'Shut the hell up,' O'Mara yelled. He fired two shots into the woodwork above their heads in a vain attempt to kill whoever was killing his men.

Shorty was now terrified. Bullets were still ripping through the wall of the saloon from the guns of the Yancys. He ran down the length of the boardwalk. When he reached the corner, he stopped.

'Bill!' he called out.

Big Bill O'Mara moved after him with both his guns raised at hip-level. When he reached the corner he saw the two men standing shoulder to shoulder a mere twenty feet away in the alley beside the saloon.

Cal Hayes and Jake Ritter were standing with their hands a few inches above their gun grips.

'If it ain't Jake Ritter. Who ya got there

with ya?' Big Bill spat at the ground between them.

'The name's Hayes, O'Mara,' the gun-fighter replied.

'Never thought we'd meet again like this, Jake.' O'Mara grinned as his thumbs pulled back on the hammers of the guns in his sweating hands.

Shorty moved closer to the doughty outlaw and raised his own guns. His hands shook almost uncontrollably.

'It was you who killed my kid brother, wasn't it, Big Bill?' Jake ground out.

'You're plumb loco, Jake. I weren't nowhere near that farmhouse,' O'Mara spat out.

'I've killed every one of the varmints who were involved in that outrage, Bill.' Jake kept watching the guns in the hands of the man he hated more than any other. 'Before they died, they all mentioned your name. You informed the Pinkerton agency that me and Frank were there and they wiped your slate clean.'

O'Mara's hands slowly began to raise his guns towards the two men opposite him.

'I still say that you're loco.'

'How much did they pay you?' Jake's voice was now like the growling of a panther. 'What was the life of my little brother worth?'

'A pretty penny, Jake.' The smile on O'Mara's face was sickening.

'They also told me that it was you who tossed that grenade through the window.' Jake raised his head and stared into the soul of the outlaw. 'It's amazing how impending death can loosen tongues.'

'It should have been you inside that house, Jake.' Big Bill laughed as the sound of his gun hammers locking filled the street.

Both Jake and Hayes went for their guns when they saw the barrels of O'Mara's weaponry aim at them and fire.

They fanned their gun hammers with their gloved hands until their pistols were red-hot and empty.

When the gunsmoke drifted away, both men stared at the dead bodies before them.

'You're fast, Hayes. Real fast,' Jake Ritter said as they both watched Frank and the

Yancy brothers rushing out of the saloon towards them.

'Not as fast as you, Jake,' Hayes admitted.

'Nobody is.'

Frank grabbed hold of his brother's shoulders and shook him hard enough to get his attention.

'We gotta get out of here, Jake. There's a posse heading here and we don't want to be around when they arrive.'

Jake smiled.

'OK, brother Frank. Get the horses and we'll ride.'

'So that's your brother?' Hayes watched the man running off in the direction they had left their horses.

Jake grinned. 'He ain't as dumb as I tell folks he is. He reads too many books though. Ain't healthy, reading too many books.'

Colt Yancy moved close to the tall gun-fighter and eyed him up and down carefully.

'You must be Hayes.'

Hayes nodded. 'That's what they call me.'

'The youngster you've been tracking is in

the saloon tied up. He's bruised but alive,' Colt said.

'Thanks.' Hayes watched as the rest of the gang headed off to round up their horses. Only Jake remained beside him, emptying his gun before reloading it.

'It would be a kindness if you could make our excuses to the posse when they arrive, Hayes.' Jake grinned. 'And maybe send them off on the wrong trail?'

'I'll do my best, but I think that they'll be more than happy just to sweep up all these dead outlaws you and your family have littered the place with.'

Cal Hayes watched as the rest of the gang rode up to them with Jake's black roan in tow.

Jake Ritter mounted and gathered up his reins.

'Ya know something, Hayes? It must be more than twelve years since me and Frank robbed our first bank in Lincoln. We were young then and it seemed exciting.'

'Maybe you ought to quit.' Hayes looked

up at the notorious outlaw's face. A face he had seen on countless wanted posters over the years.

'Reckon it's a tad too late to quit.' Jake glanced at the bodies on the boardwalk. 'That's the way we'll all end up. Only death will end this for me.'

Cal Hayes licked his dry lips.

'I'm not going to argue with you, Jake.'

'Don't forget to pay that little lady a visit before you take that youngster back to El Paso, Hayes.'

Before Cal Hayes could reply, the outlaws had galloped off into the crimson rays of the setting sun. As he stepped up on to the boardwalk of the saloon he heard the sound of approaching riders. When he turned, he saw Rose looking at him. She still had her hands on her hips, but this time she was smiling.

Hayes touched the brim of his Stetson.

FINALE

The streets of El Paso shimmered in the afternoon sun. An almost blinding heat haze blurred the wide street from prying eyes as the two horsemen slowly rode between the white sun-bleached buildings towards the bank.

People stopped and studied the weary riders. The blood on the clothes of the pair had long since dried but lost none of its gruesome reality.

It was obvious that Cal Hayes and Joseph McCabe had been in a battle which had cost them dearly. They were slumped in their saddles and were allowing their mounts to find their own pace up towards the imposing building.

Without speaking, both men pulled back on their reins at exactly the same moment.

They paused and then slowly dismounted, as if every movement racked their bodies in unimaginable agony. It had been a long and exhausting ride.

Cal Hayes looped his reins around the hitching pole and watched as his travelling companion did the same.

Both men stepped up on to the board-walk, then paused.

Joseph McCabe looked at the face of the man beside him and smiled. It was the first time he had been able to smile since Big Bill and his cronies had abducted him.

'You OK?' Hayes asked the younger man.

'Are you?'

The gunfighter grinned.

'I've been a lot better but at least I got you back alive.'

The door of the bank swung open and Rufas McCabe came rushing out into the blazing sunshine. He grabbed his son and sobbed into the shoulder of his only child.

Cal Hayes watched the heartbreaking scene silently.

It seemed strange to him. Yet he had no knowledge of what it felt like to have anyone who cared for him that way. He had been alone for as long as he could recall.

Without uttering a word, Hayes turned away. He left the father and son to celebrate their reunion alone.

Then a hand caught his shoulder, stopping him in his tracks. Hayes's head turned. He stared at the banker.

Hayes had never seen tears in the eyes of a banker before.

'What, Mr McCabe?'

Rufas McCabe swallowed hard and managed to speak to the man who had restored his faith.

'I owe you a bonus, Hayes. A very big bonus. You brought my son back alive.'

The gunfighter looked at Joseph McCabe and then at his doting father. For the first time in his life he envied someone.

'You don't owe me anything,' Hayes said, patting the breast pocket of his denim jacket. 'A Pinkerton man gave me a receipt for the bounty on Big Bill O'Mara and his gang. I'll be fine once it's cashed.'

'Are you sure?' Rufas McCabe asked.

Hayes paused. 'If I were you, though, I'd keep a sharp eye out for the Ritter–Yancy gang. I've got me an inkling that they might be in these parts.'

'Thank you, Mr Hayes.' McCabe nodded.

'No problem.'

Both men watched the gunfighter step back down into the street and walk across its shimmering sand towards the nearest of El Paso's many saloons.

Then, as Hayes rested his boot on the boardwalk opposite he glanced back at them and smiled. It was the broadest smile either man had ever witnessed. Hayes then thought about the stubborn female named Rose and wondered whether it was worth returning to that remote town one day.

Cal Hayes touched the brim of his Stetson and then continued into the saloon. He had earned the right to quench the thirst that took him in through the swing doors.

The publishers hope that this book has given you enjoyable reading. Large Print Books are especially designed to be as easy to see and hold as possible. If you wish a complete list of our books please ask at your local library or write directly to:

Dales Large Print Books
Magna House, Long Preston,
Skipton, North Yorkshire.
BD23 4ND

This Large Print Book, for people
who cannot read normal print,
is published under the auspices of
THE ULVERSCROFT FOUNDATION